Dan Johnson's Ashes

Sequel to
The Secret of the Spring

Garry Leeson

Dan Johnson's Ashes
© 2023 Garry Leeson

Cover design: Rebekah Wetmore
Editor: Andrew Wetmore
ISBN: 978-1-990187-50-6
First edition October, 2023

Moose House Publications
2475 Perotte Road
Annapolis County, NS
B0S 1A0
moosehousepress.com
info@moosehousepress.com

We live and work in Mi'kma'ki, the ancestral and unceded territory of the Mi'kmaw people. This territory is covered by the "Treaties of Peace and Friendship" which Mi'kmaw and Wolastoqiyik (Maliseet) people first signed with the British Crown in 1725. The treaties did not deal with surrender of lands and resources but in fact recognized Mi'kmaq and Wolastoqiyik (Maliseet) title and established the rules for what was to be an ongoing relationship between nations. We are all Treaty people.

Also by Garry Leeson

The Dome Chronicles (Nevermore Press)
   Winner of the 2021 Margaret & John Savage First
   Book (nonfiction) Atlantic Book Award

The Secret of the Spring (Moose House)
   The earlier adventures of Dan Johnson's family

For
Brenden, Timothy. Zoe and Emily
and, of course,
Andrea

This is a work of fiction. The author has created the characters, conversations, interactions, and events; and any
resemblance of any character to any real person, apart
from historical references, is coincidental.

Dan Johnson's Ashes

Dan Johnson's Ashes

1: What do you say to that?

Dan Johnson, or, as the old man often joked, all that remained of him, stood staring out the window of his room on the fourth floor of the Veterans' Centre of Toronto's Sunnybrook Hospital. The view from that window had recently become a source of confusion to him. Sometimes when he looked down over the Don Valley, with its meandering brook and wooded verges, that's all he would see.

But often, too often these days, his thoughts would slide and he would be standing on the brow of Nova Scotia's North Mountain, looking down over a patchwork of small farms nestled along the Annapolis River. He even imagined he could see the roof of the house where he was born and the plume of smoke coming from the blacksmith shop beside it.

It was that old photograph that his grandson, Alex, had given him that started Dan on these trips into the past. Alex had lovingly had the old sepia restored, enlarged and framed. In it a group of two women, two men and two young boys stood posing in front of a blacksmith shop—Ben's shop.

As a matter of convenience, Dan Johnson always identified the people in the photo as being himself;

his mother, Lilly; his father, Ben; his Uncle Alphonse; his Aunt Angie and their son, Tommy. In fact, only Lilly was truly his mother. The rest were simply assumed relationships forged out of abiding love and respect. Ben, despite his lack of paternal credentials, was and would always be his father.

A shake of his head snapped Dan out of his reverie and back into the present.

He had things to do. There was something about today that he was supposed to remember. The nurse had hinted about today being special when she brought in his breakfast. Whatever was going on, he thought he better be ready.

He dug a new white shirt out of a drawer, chuckling to himself as he remembered the old joke about one more white shirt should see the old bugger out. *Too true, too true!*

He had just wrestled himself into the shirt when an orderly came barging into the room with Dan's freshly pressed blue Legion blazer over his arm. He accepted the man's help with the jacket and knotting his regimental tie.

Once he was gone, Dan moved over to the wall mirror. He adjusted his medals and service ribbons and started running a comb through his thinning white hair.

As always, he was shocked by the withered image that confronted him when he dared to look at his reflection. He remembered Ben saying that, no matter how old he got, whenever he first looked into a mirror, he expected to see an eighteen-year-old boy.

Where now was the handsome young boy who had once looked down over the Valley?

Where now was the proud soldier and policeman he had once been?

Now they only resided in the photos mounted on the wall on either side of his grandson's gift.

"Sans eyes, sans teeth, sans everything." That's how Ben would have put it. Ben had a saying or a quotation for almost everything.

But what the hell! All in all, Dan had had a pretty good life and was set up to live the remainder of it in style, with a room all of his own, twenty-four seven care, a doting grandson and a cluster of medals and ribbons acknowledging what he had accomplished in a distant past.

He was busy pinning a final medal on his jacket when there was a quiet knock and then the door burst open and the room filled with a host of grinning white clad nurses and orderlies, followed by fellow patients in dressing gowns and slippers.

"Happy birthday to you, happy birthday to you, happy birthday, dear Danny, happy birthday to you!"

Dan's grandson, Alex, was holding the cake. Bill, a British veteran who had made himself ranking officer of the floor, elbowed him aside, assumed a commanding position and commenced the proceedings. "Now, Danny boy, don't be disappointed that there's only one candle on the cake. The fire marshal would not have approved of the appropriate number. A hell of a hazard, what!"

As Alex moved the cake with its beckoning single

candle closer to his grandfather, Bill, fumbling and digging into his pockets, interrupted again. "Hold your fire while I read you this greeting from a very special admirer. Where the devil did I put my...? Here, lend me those glasses...Ah, that's better...It says here, 'I am pleased to know that you are celebrating your 100th birthday. I send my congratulations and best wishes to you on such a special occasion.'"

He looked up with a grim glint in his eye. "And there it is, old boy, the Queen's signature. And what do you say to that? I think a speech is in order."

Dan quickly blew out the candle and turned back to Bill. "Here's what I say, you pompous old prick. I think my grandson should stay with me, but the rest of you should get out of here and take that cake with you."

2: Is that smoke?

Alex followed the offended parties into the hall.

"I'm sorry, folks. It must be one of his bad days. Why don't you all go down to the cafeteria and have your coffee and cake there."

In the old man's waning years, his grandfather's preference for directness had crystallized into the succinct, abrasive manner in which he now addressed things that didn't quite suit him and Alex was frequently obliged to make excuses.

He had gone directly to Head Nurse Jessiman a month earlier, when he saw that his grandfather's temper was getting out of hand, but she had immediately dismissed his entreaties.

"Save your breath, young man. None of us are offended by your grandfather's rants—in fact, we kind of look forward to them. It brings a little colour into our lives. He hasn't fooled us, and I presume that you must also know that inside that cantankerous shell dwells a thoughtful, sweet, generous man. See those flowers at the nurses' station? Those are Irma's; it's her birthday and who do you think sent them to her? Your grandfather got me to give him a list of the birthdays of everybody on the ward and these bouquets are popping up all the time. Sam, the orderly, had his bicycle stolen a while ago and somehow a replacement miraculously appeared in our bike racks two days later. Some of the staff say that they saw a police van with the Mounted Unit insignia delivering it. Everybody knows he was a legend in the department and I suppose he is still in a position to call in favours. Don't let him fool you. There's nothing that he enjoys more than what he refers to as the pissing matches you and he get into, so don't let up on him."

"I don't relish fighting with him every time we talk."

"One of our psychologists suggests that your grandfather's attitude is just a defence mechanism: a way to keep his true self to himself," Nurse Jessiman said. "The doctor thinks that the condition is a result of PTSD and that he might be able to help him. I say, leave well enough alone. For god's sake, the man is going to be one hundred years old shortly. I have spent over twenty-five years working in palliative care wards and I've learned that the solution to all the patients' problems is obvious, constantly imminent and just a matter of time. My beeper goes off and I must go in and close the eyes of someone whose hang-ups and worries have all gone away. I know this sounds crass and unfeeling but I need you to know that, now that his time is limited, he needs you more than ever. You're all he's got, and I know he loves you."

All the hospital staff was understanding—they knew that patients with dementia often experienced radical personality changes, and even gentle, quiet people could become rude and aggressive.

Alex stood watching the group of downtrodden revellers disappear down the hall, steeling himself before reentering the room.

His grandfather was standing, staring out the window. "Come here, Alex. Look down there. Is that smoke?"

"I don't see any smoke, Gramps. Come over and sit down. We need to talk. Why did you hold back, Gramps? Why didn't you tell them how you really felt? You are one cranky old bastard these days, but I love you all the same. Jesus! I couldn't believe the looks on their faces."

"Well, maybe I was a little short, son, but that old bastard from next door really gets on my nerves. I haven't liked British officers since they lorded over me during the war. Anyway he's a real blowhard, always going on about what he did in World War Two. That was hardly a war compared to the big one, and anyway if you ask anybody here about their experiences in any war, they won't want to talk about it. Bragging is a sure sign of someone who never did more than man a desk."

"I know, I know, Gramps. You tell me the same thing every time I try to pry something out of you. I'm not going to bug you anymore about your experiences in the war or the police force. I know better."

He took a breath, then plunged in. "But there's a whole lot about our family history that I do want to know about. You've been pretty tight-lipped about our family connections back in Nova Scotia. If I hadn't found that old photo and forced you to tell me who was in it, I wouldn't even know the little I know now. Why are you so secretive about it? You would never speak about it with Grandma, and my dad went to his grave knowing almost nothing of your past."

"It's like Ben always said: 'Sonny, it's best to let sleeping dogs lie.'"

"For Christ's sake, Gramps, it's always Ben, Ben this, Ben that. You've been referencing some wise old man named Ben for as long as I remember, but until I dug up that old photo and squeezed the information out of you, I never knew who he was. I think you owe it to me to share a little bit more about your past."

The old man rose stiffly to his feet and waddled over to his bed, lay down and then spoke in a breathy tone. "Maybe you're right, son, but I'm really tired right now so I'm gonna get some sleep. The next time you visit, remind me and we'll talk a bit more about it. Anyway, I've got some other import-ant things to run by you, so, for now, piss off and let me get some rest."

3: Mumbo jumbo

"What the hell is this?"

Dan Johnson was sitting in a wheelchair beside his window. He lifted a framed certificate and waggled it at his grandson.

"Nice way to greet your only living relative, you sour old bastard."

"I'll repeat. What the hell is this?"

"Hand it over and I'll have a look."

Alex tilted the certificate to catch the light from the window and read, "This is to certify that Dan Johnson has agreed to participate in the Valour Project."

"What the hell is the Valour Project? I didn't volunteer to participate in anything. Ben advised us when we shipped out that we should never volunteer for anything—probably saved my life. I've never volunteered for anything since, not in the army, not on the police force, not anywhere. I sure as hell didn't volunteer for whatever this is."

"Let me explain, Gramps. The Valour Project is a study a bunch of well-intentioned eggheads have come up with to try to determine whether there is a correlation between a person's DNA and his propensity to bravery."

"Spare me all that mumbo jumbo and tell me what the hell is going on here."

"It's like this, Gramps. The project has collected and banked DNA samples from thousands of decorated heroes from all over the world. I'm not sure why, but it might be a tool to do selective recruiting. I guess I should have told you about this."

"Damn certain you should have!"

"Anyway, last summer when you had one of your spells and you were unconscious for so long, I thought it might be the big one and I was going to lose you. So, when the Valour folks came around collecting samples, I gave the okay. I guess I thought I would be preserving a little piece of you."

"You're breaking my bloody heart, you sentimental sap. I didn't agree to give that sample and I want it back. How did they take the sample, anyway? I was lying there helpless. I've always worried about what those horny nurses were up to when I was in that state."

"Listen, Gramps, I'm sure that, despite the temptation that your vibrant, sensuous body presents, the nurses are able to control themselves. As to the matter of getting that sample back, I'll have to look into the matter. Now, can we get on to some more important matters?"

4: C'mon, boy

"Good, you're here. Did you take Jack for his walk?"

Oh, Jesus, here we go again, Alex thought as he moved over and sat down on a chair close to where the old man lay on his bed. Speaking more abruptly than he intended, he said, "C'mon, Gramps, Jack died a long time ago. Try to remember."

This thing about the dog had started a year earlier. They had been on one of their monthly visits to Dan's house, where Alex was staying because it was close to the university. It was the one occasion when Dan had allowed Alex to take the old man's precious vintage pickup truck out of the garage and bring it over to the hospital to drive him.

Alex always kept the truck keys in his pocket when he went to the ward and helped him down to where it was waiting because Dan would invariably scramble up into the driver's seat. He would sit there for a moment, holding the steering wheel and testing the feel of the clutch and the brake before reluctantly sliding along the bench seat to the passenger side.

When they got to the house, it was always more an inspection tour than a visit. Alex had busied himself making a pot of tea while Dan made the rounds making sure everything was precisely as he had left it.

"Tea is ready, Gramps. Come and get it while it's hot."

The old man complied, but instead of moving directly to his chair by the kitchen table, he walked over to the back door, opened it and started calling.

"Here, Jack, here! Jack, c'mon boy, c'mon boy."

Alex sat stunned, letting the old man continue for a few moments before getting up and going to him. He had put his hand on the confused man's shoulder and began the first of many attempts to explain things to him.

"Jack was a good old dog, Gramps. But remember, he passed away a long time ago. Come and drink your tea. It'll perk you up."

The incident had repeated itself several times before the old man's worsening condition made their brief trips home no longer possible.

Alex understood his grandfather's strange attachment to a dog that no longer existed. He had known Jack himself when he was very young, and the dog had been truly exceptional, and probably worthy of being immortalized in this strange manner.

Jack had been a police dog before Dan adopted him. Word had come to him from the Canine Squad that one of their best dogs had gone rogue and dangerous after a serious incident and was scheduled for euthanasia. Dan insisted that he have a chance to rehabilitate the German Shepherd, and the powers that be complied. Jack would be the fourth retired police dog that Dan had made a home for.

It was the same with retired police horses. Dan had provided a loving final home for his own personal mount when he became redundant, and over the years there was a succession of cast-off police horses that had found a safe place with him. When he applied to acquire one of the older mounts no one had the nerve to say 'no' to famous 'Inspector Dan' of the Mounted Unit.

But Jack was long gone and Major, his last police horse retiree, had passed away twenty years ago. Dan had gone for his last ride on Major, with Jack alongside, on his eightieth birthday.

5: The only one left

"Gramps, can we talk about what's going on in this picture? I want to know these people. You've said who they are but that's all I know about them so far."

"I said I'd fill you in a bit, son, and I guess this is as good a time as any, so fire away with your questions."

"Let's start with your mum, Lilly. She looks so young."

"She was young. I look to be about ten years old in that picture. That would make her twenty five."

"What about Ben? He's in good shape, but a lot older than your mum."

"I always thought of Ben as ageless, but you're right. He was a lot older than Mum."

"How much older?"

"I'm not sure, but I figure that when that picture was taken he was about sixty-five."

"You always refer to him as your father. But he really wasn't, was he?"

"Watch what you say, boy! You keep talking like that and this interview is coming to an end! Ben Johnson was more of a father to me than anybody else could have been."

"Sorry, Gramps, I know by the way that you are always referring to his words of wisdom that you have the greatest respect for him. Let's talk about the other man in the picture. What was his name again —Alphonse, or something like that?"

"Alphonse Arseneau and, aside from Ben, he was the kindest most intelligent man I have ever known. His son, Tommy, was my best friend—more like a brother to me."

"That just leaves the other woman in the picture. You call her Aunt Angie. What was her story?"

"Come to think of it, I don't think I ever knew her family name. Her front name was Angeline and she was Angeline Arseneau after she married Alphonse."

"So now I'm wondering how all these people fit into your life and what ever became of them."

"Well, for starters, I'm the only one left out of the group. They've all been dead or disappeared for as long as I can remember. Ben and Alphonse were best friends, as were my mother and Angie. My mum and Angie met while working as maids in the Spa Springs Hotel. Tommy and I grew up together and did everything together, working on the farm, wintering in the woods and serving together in the army."

"And?"

Dan shrugged. "I don't know about Tommy. The others are buried on the mountain behind the home place."

"Grampy, I still can't help but wonder, if Ben wasn't your real father, who was?"

"That did it, Sonny! I warned you. This interview

is over, so piss off!"

6: Words of wisdom

"Is it safe to come in here?"

Alex was peering through the partially opened door of his grandfather's room.

"Get in here! Where the hell have you been?"

"Well, Gramps, the way things ended up the last time I was here, I thought it would be better if I laid low for a bit."

"Well, you thought wrong," The old man shouted. Then he said in a softer tone, "There's still a hell of a lot that we have to get at while we still can. Where were you yesterday? I called the house and there was no answer."

"You know what yesterday was. That's the day we always visit Dad, Mum and Grandma's graves. I was there. I told them that you were busy and couldn't make it."

"I should have been there with you. Did you get the flowers?"

"Same as every year, same florist, same flowers."

"Good, now why are you dancing around? What's on your mind? Spit it out."

Alex took a step back to be further out of range while he thought about what he wanted to say.

"While I was visiting with Grandma and Dad, I realized that you and I have never discussed what you want done when the time comes. There are no arrangements and no plans. Nobody will know what to do."

"Now that's funny. I remember presenting a similar dilemma to Ben before Tommy and I shipped out. Do you know what he told me?"

"No, I don't, but I feel more of Ben's words of wisdom coming on."

"Ben told me that I shouldn't worry about what would happen when he died. His exact words were, 'If you lie around stinking long enough, somebody will come along and bury you.'"

"Come on, Gramps, be serious. I really need to know."

The old man shuffled around the room before settling into the old stuffed chair that he had insisted on bringing from his home. He turned to Alex. "You better write this down. First, I don't want to end up in a coffin six feet in the ground. I want to be cremated. Yes, yes, I know I've got that expensive plot at Mount Pleasant paid for and the funeral parlour has already gouged the prepaid expenses out of me, but this is what I want: I want you to take the urn with my ashes and have it buried in that spacious plot beside the rest. But before you do, I want you to take most of the ashes out of the urn. Put them in a can or a box —anything handy."

"Are you kidding me? What are you talking about?"

"I stopped kidding some time ago. Now listen to what I'm saying. I want you to take those ashes to the old home place in Nova Scotia. There's a small graveyard on the slope above the house. I'd like you to spread them there."

7: Lazy lawyer

"Bring me that folder, Alex."

Dan took the cheap cardboard container, removed the elastic, then took out the contents and spread them on the small table he used for his meals when he didn't feel like eating in the cafeteria.

"Pull up a chair and sit beside me. I've got some important things to show you and some serious business to discuss."

"Am I in trouble?"

"I play the fool around here. What do the actors say? 'Leave 'em laughing'. I haven't much time left and I guess that's what I'm trying to do. It's a pity that the folks around here don't have the sense of humour that you do."

Alex dragged his chair over by the bed.

"Yesterday a doctor came in to see me. He said that the nurses were concerned because I frequently woke up with nightmares and that he thought that I might have PTSD. I pretended to be offended and informed him in no uncertain terms that I had never had any form of venereal disease. He just looked puzzled and walked away mumbling to himself.

"But you know that most of my life has been a

serious affair—not a hell of a lot to laugh about. So let's go over this stuff. This is everything I had in the strong box at the bank."

Dan picked up a document with a red ribbon around it. "Let's start with the will. Nothing too surprising there: you're my only heir so the whole kit and caboodle will be yours when I kick off. I could go on about what I want you to do with the stuff, but I won't be around to check so I imagine you'll do whatever you want to—you always have."

He passed the document over. "This is your copy. Never mind reading it now. Take it home and go over it and savour all the loot you're going to get."

He picked up a little pile of papers. "Here is the deed for the house in the city and another for the cottage, but here is another one you might not know about. I was a little surprised myself when it came with some other documents long after I sold all my holdings in Nova Scotia. Apparently my home property was in two pieces, and part of it wasn't included in the sale of the land around the house and the blacksmith shop. When the lazy lawyer who was looking after the matter finally got around to sending this deed, he included this."

Dan fumbled with an arthritic hand to dislodge a yellowed document from the pages that concealed it and passed it over.

"What's this? Wow, a marriage certificate. Is this what I think it is?" Alex peered at it. "It's not yours...it's too old."

Suddenly he pointed at a line near the top of the

document. "My god, this is your parents' marriage license."

8: What a bunch of nonsense!

"Okay, Sonny, tell me again what those courses are at U of T that you've been spending all my hard-earned money on."

"English Lit with a major in poetry," Alex said. "And I haven't used a cent of that trust fund money you're so worried about. I've been paying my own way, slaving away at that stable in the valley."

"Ah-hah! I remember now. That's why you come staggering in here at all hours smelling of horseshit."

"As I recall you spent most of your life smelling of horseshit when you were on the Mounted Unit."

Dan waved a dismissive hand. "More about this course you're taking. Did you say poetry?"

"Here we go again. Yes, I said poetry."

"Well, why don't you give me a little example of what you've been working on? You know, recite a poem for me. Here, I'll start one for you. 'Roses are red, Violets are blue.' You finish it, Sonny."

"Very funny."

"Yes, it is funny. It's funny how things turn out sometimes. I'm remembering something Ben said when he was trying to talk Tommy and me into not going into the army."

"Ben again; okay, lay it on me."

"Ben was quoting a guy named Adams, who said, 'I am a warrior so that my son may be a merchant, so that his son may be a poet.' Tell me that that doesn't ring true. Tommy and I defied Ben and went off to that stupid war, your father worked himself into an early grave trying to keep that business of his afloat, and now here you are scratching out poems. By the way, how did you get that black eye you're sporting? Not the kind of thing I expect to see on poet."

Alex rubbed his eye self-consciously. "Thanks for noticing. You should see the other guy."

"I want a full report."

"I got into a bit of a tussle with a guy down at the stable. He claimed I was paying too much attention to his girlfriend, who's in one of the riding classes."

"And were you?"

"That's the thing: I still don't know. There are so many girls around there and I try to give them all my attention!"

"Stop your bragging and tell me what happened."

"The guy jumped me from behind, spun me around and landed one punch before I could use the stuff you taught me."

Dan shook his head. "I taught you that it was a poor set of legs that let your nose get in trouble."

"But you also taught me not to take shit from anybody, so I didn't."

Alex put a hand on his grandfather's arm. "Anyway, you certainly saved my butt yesterday. I would have looked a hell of a lot worse than this if I hadn't remembered the story that Dad told me about you and him at the CNE when he was a kid."

"What the hell are you talking about?"

"He told me that one day, when he was about ten years old, he went to meet you at the Horse Palace. He said you had stabled your horse, changed into civilian clothes and was taking him for a walk around the midway. He said you had promised to take him for a ride on the Ferris wheel, but that never happened. You noticed something going on behind one of the carnival tents and you and he went over to investigate.

Dan was frowning as if trying to remember.

"There had been a brawl going on and several men and one woman were injured. They were cowering away from a huge man who stood beating his chest and growling, 'Who else wants me, who else wants me? Come on!' Dad said he thinks he was the strongman from one of the side shows."

"What a bunch of nonsense!"

"Dad said that you casually walked up and confronted the behemoth who then turned his attention to you.

"'So you want me, do ya?' he bellowed over and over, shaking his fist and ready to swing.

"Dad said you ducked a couple of punches then stepped back, holding your hands in the air. But then, and this the best part, you pointed over his shoulder and said, 'I don't want you, but that guy behind you seems to.'

"The big jerk turned around to see who was there

and, when he looked back, the last thing he saw was the bunched knuckles of your flying fist.

"Dad said the man dropped like a pole-axed hog and you went over and helped the woman to her feet. Then you took her hand and you both walked away, leaving the unconscious man where he landed. Dad said he asked you if you were going to arrest the man, but you just said, 'No.'

"Dad said, every time he told that story, he wondered why you just walked away and every time I heard it, I wondered the same. So, why didn't arrest him, Gramps?"

"If that's a true story, and I doubt it is," Dan said, "the answer is simple. Those were different times, simple times. Cops walked their beat or rode their horses and they were known by everyone in their area and the cops knew almost all the bad apples. For the most part, bullies and wife beaters were dealt with summarily. We called it 'cursory justice.' If your Dad's recollection is accurate it was an example of the police service reducing court time and saving tax payers an unnecessary burden."

"I love it, Gramps," Alex said. "The reason I brought it up is because I used that old trick of yours yesterday. 'Who's that behind you?' I said to the guy was beating on me and, bang, that was the end of him."

Alex looked at the clock on the bedside table and realized that visiting hours were over. "I've got to go now so I better finish that poem you started for me.

Roses are red
Violets are blue
I don't take shit
I'm just like you!

See you soon, Gramps."

9: You've lost me

"What are you dragging in here now?"

"It's your album and scrapbook, Gramps," Alex said.

"Didn't know I had one."

"Your memory isn't that bad. I dug this out of Dad's stuff. Gramma kept this going for years and it's got some really great photos and newspaper clippings in it. You and I are going to have a look in this together."

"You look at it, Sonny," Dan said. "I've seen it all. Take it back home with you."

"What's the matter with you? I'm not taking it anywhere. I'm leaving it right here in your room so other people can look in it and see that you weren't always the cranky old bastard you let on to being now. I want people to know who you really are."

"Good luck with that. I don't even know who I really am, and if I don't, neither do you."

"You've lost me, Gramps."

Dan sighed. "You made a big deal the other day out of the fact that I didn't know who my father was. That means that your father didn't know who his grandfather was and you don't know who your great-grandfather was. So, none of us really know where we came from and who we really are."

"Thanks for finally confiding that bit of information, Gramps, but I don't think it's anything to lose sleep over."

"Funny you should say that, because I have had a nightmare my whole life. When it happens, I'm just a kid again, standing with Tommy in front of a store. Somebody comes out and is about to say something but then I wake up and I never know what they say. Gramma used to tell me that I would wake up yelling, 'tell me, tell me.' I still wake up yelling sometimes. The idiot doctor here thinks it's PTSD from the war but it's nothing of the kind. I know that much for sure."

10: You've finally done it

Alex listened to the message on the house phone. It was the message he dreaded but knew was coming. His grandfather's fainting spells had worsened and become more frequent recently, and now the doctor was confirming his worst fears.

"Bad news, Alex. Your grandfather is in a deep coma. I've moved him into the ICU. When you get this message, get here as soon as possible."

Alex immediately called for a cab.

He had been away for two days and that phone call was already twenty-four hours old. He had a good excuse for not being there in the daytime, but not the nights. *Those damned final exams, but who am I kidding? That explains the days but not the two nights I spent at the Sorority with Ann.*

He encouraged the taxi driver to make the best time possible, promising a good tip.

Arriving, he jumped out and ran, propelled by his guilt, taking the familiar steps leading to the Veterans' Wing two at a time. He continued running past the reception area and down the hall to his grandfather's room.

The door was open and, except for a bed and a

few other items of standard hospital furniture, the room was empty. He went over to the closet and opened the door.

"Christ, they've taken everything out."

He stood staring blindly into the empty closet until he felt a hand on his shoulder.

Nurse Jessiman guided him over to the bed, sat him down on the edge and started to explain. "Your grandfather is up in ICU and I'm sorry, but the doctors say that there is no way he will recover and come back. We've put all his things in a safe place and you can pick them up whenever you want."

"What are you saying? Is he, is he…?"

"No, dear, he hasn't passed away yet. But you better get yourself up there. Just remember he probably won't be able to speak, but he can hear and understand everything you say. I liked your idea of keeping his scrapbook beside him so that everybody who attends him will know who he is, so I sent it up with him."

Alex was grateful for the clear signs. His brain was churning too hard to let him figure out the way to the ICU by himself. It seemed an endless time of walking and waiting for elevators, but finally he was standing beside the bed his grandfather was lying in. *His last bed.*

"Well, Gramps, you've finally done it. You've gone and got yourself so sick you can't move or speak. I'll admit it, I was out in the hall crying for five minutes before I manned up and came in here. But I got to thinking—I've got the old bugger right where I want him. I can say whatever I want and you can't tell me to shut the fuck up. You know what we're going to do? We're going to go through that old album of yours so that I can remind you that you aren't the old dickhead that you've been pretending to be. I wish I could ask you to blink or wag a finger when you agree with what I show or tell you, but the doctors tell me that that won't be possible so you'll just have to lie there and listen."

He hefted the old album. "There're lots of old photos in here, but we both know about most of them. I want to talk to you about the newspaper clippings that Gramma saved. Take this one, for example."

Alex opened the album to one of the first pages. "This is a *Toronto Star* article with a photo of a line of twelve mounted policemen in the Santa Claus parade."

He flipped through the pages, "There are a dozen photos like this in here. You must have led the parade every year. And I really like this one in the *Toronto Telegram*. You're standing beside your horse and the horse has a robber pinned against a store window. The paper says that the horse's name was Joe. I remember Joe; you once let me ride him. There's a picture of me on him somewhere in here. Here's another picture of you from the *Globe and Mail*: you're leading your horse through a crowd at the CNE Midway and you've got a child in your arms. It says he was lost and you found him."

He picked up a snapshot, loose among the clippings. "Wow! Here's one of Gram's photos of you and me working on your log cabin. You worked me like a hired mule that summer. I thought I'd never get all those logs peeled."

Alex put down the album and hauled a chair over so he could sit down. He felt remarkably tired for the guy in the room who wasn't dying. When he was set, he picked up the album again.

"Here's one of you driving that old horse you borrowed to skid the logs out. The guy who owned the horse was reluctant to lend him to a city slicker like you, but after seeing the way you handled him, I remember he said, 'If you ever want to give up your job on the Police Department, you can come up here and work in the woods with me.' That was a wonderful time, Gramps. I learned so much from you."

There was a gasping sound. Alex closed the album, leaned closer, and took his grandfather's hand.

The old man's eyes shot open for an instant, then closed again, a tear running down his cheek. His lips were moving. He seemed to be trying to speak. Alex leaned in closer to listen to Dan Johnson's last whispered words.

"Tell me...Tell me...Tell..."

The emergency nurse rushed in as the rhythmic bleeping of the monitor settled into a constant whine.

11: From the obituary

Inspector Daniel Johnson, formerly of the Toronto Police Department, passed away peacefully at the Sunnybrook Veterans' Hospital on March fourth of this year. Inspector Dan, as his colleagues referred to him, was one hundred years old. He was an often-decorated veteran of WWI, having served with distinction on several fronts including Passchendaele, Ypres and Vimy Ridge. He reenlisted in 1939 and served as a commissioned officer with 13 Hussars until he was declared essential and was called back to head the Toronto Police Mounted Unit. He was a well-known figure in the streets of Toronto...

12: Poutine

Alex nursed the old pickup truck out of the centre of the city, being extra careful when he switched gears. If his grandfather was up there somewhere listening, as well as being in the can on the seat beside him, he didn't want him to hear the old gearbox grinding.

"Grind me another pound!" his grandfather used to yell when he was teaching Alex to drive.

When he finally hit the 401 and the open road heading east, he felt more comfortable. He lifted his foot and released the clutch, then patted the steering wheel.

Mostly high gear from now on, old girl.

As he cruised along, Alex mulled over the events of the last two weeks. He had been overwhelmed by the shock and then the persistent grief over the loss of his grandfather, followed by the bittersweet knowledge that at the old man's passing, he had become a millionaire.

What the hell am I thinking? Make that a multi-millionaire. If the lawyer and the appraiser were correct, Gramps' place on Cowan Ave. where he had spent most of his life paying off his fifteen thousand dollar mortgage, was now worth over a million dollars and Dad's house should be worth slightly more. And then there was the lakeside log cottage on prime vacation land.

I hope the tenants will take good care of those houses for now. I guess I could keep one and sell the other. Lots of time to figure that out later. For the moment, I have to look after what Gramps asked me to do.

His decision to take the old truck was a good one. He had had so much time in it, sitting beside his grandfather on their trips up to the cabin, that, even if he hadn't had his ashes sitting next to him, he still would have felt Gramps' presence and been comfortable talking with him.

Reaching over and patting the old tobacco can, a relic from his grandfather's roll-your-own days, he asked, "So, how do you like riding shotgun now, Gramps? Not as much fun as driving, is it? I hope you're okay with me taking your truck, you silly old bugger. What else was I supposed to do? Your advice to take the CNR train to Halifax and then switch to the DAR for the rest of the way to Middleton kind of fell apart when I found out that they tore out the DAR tracks in 1985. Jesus... that hotel you recommended, The American House, hasn't been in operation since 1950 and they tore it down in 1960. I could have flown to Halifax and rented a car, but not to worry, this old truck and I are getting along just fine."

The pickup wasn't the gas guzzler that Alex had expected—only a couple of stops to fill it up, grab a snack and use the washroom before entering Quebec. He was making good time, maybe too good. It was still rush hour when he reached Montreal and found himself inching through the city at a snail's pace.

He abandoned his plan to get some authentic poutine while he was there—the traffic and noise were too much. He had to get out of there. As soon as a clear way to the beckoning eastbound highway presented itself, he took it.

I'm out of here toute de suite. Maybe I'll get poutine on the way back.

He wanted to put as much distance as he could between him and that chaotic home of the Habs before nightfall.

He had his headlights turned on for an hour or so before he decided that it was time to find somewhere to eat and put his head down. Presently a sleazy-looking motel announced its presence with a huge, flashing neon sign. He wasn't sure what it said but some of the graphics suggested that there might food available and he was really hungry, so he decided to hit the restaurant first and check in later.

The number of cars in the parking lot suggested that he might have accidentally come upon a popular eatery. Locking the truck, he headed to the entrance.

As soon as he opened the door an overpowering cloud of cigarette smoke greeted him. and the intensity of the throbbing base line of a rock song being belted out in what he assumed was French almost drove him backwards out of the building.

Alex turned to leave, but a very large, slick-looking fellow grabbed his arm and, smiling, seemed to be trying to direct him to a table. Alex made a couple of attempts to dissuade him but his language skills were not up to the task, so he let himself be ushered over and seated.

He was looking down at the menu when he sensed someone hovering near his shoulder. *Jesus, I hope whoever it is speaks English. I can't make any of this stuff out.*

A slender arm holding utensils wrapped in a paper napkin moved around him and put the neat package in front of him. When he turned his head to thank her he found himself staring into two huge, flaccid, naked breasts. They were only inches away!

And then, "What would you like, sir?"

All he could think of was two poached eggs, but out of caution decided not to test her sense of humour. He requested the poutine he had forgone in Montreal instead.

The meal was as good as the band was bad. There must have been a repeat sign on the score they were using for Stairway to Heaven, because he had long since finished his chips, gravy and cheese and they were still at it.

When one of the waitresses joined the band and started butchering a Céline Dion song, Alex had had enough. He left cash and a sizable tip on the table and headed for the door.

He walked out past the flashing vacancy sign and over to the truck, first checking to see that the huge metal chest resting in the open back was still locked and undisturbed. Then he opened the driver side door, slid in and patted the tobacco can.

"You really missed a good one there, Gramps. Considering some of those magazines I found when I cleared out your things, you would have enjoyed it. I'm going to pass on getting a room here, I think. I'll find a suitable spot up ahead and we'll pull over and get some zzz's right here in the cab."

As he turned the truck toward the highway, Alex made a mental note of the flashing French words on the lofty sign: *Serveuses aux Seins Nus*. He'd have to remember those for his next time through the area.

13: Stowaway

Alex woke to the loud *rat-tat* sound of a semi-trailer truck motor-braking as it descended the steep hill on the highway. When he'd pulled over into the roadside picnic area, he thought that he was going to have a quick catnap and then press on through the night. But when he climbed stiffly out of the truck and checked his watch, he realized he had been slumped over the steering wheel for six hours.

Leaving the truck door open, he moved over to the edge of the campsite and relieved himself, chuckling at his grandfather's favourite admonishment, "If you shake it more than three times...you're playing with it."

He was still a bit groggy as he made his way back to the truck. He had one foot on the running board, about to swing in, when he noticed something and quickly stepped back.

In the brief time he had been away attending to the call of nature he had acquired a passenger. A young German Shepherd dog had pushed his granddad's can aside and was sitting on the passenger side of the bench seat.

"What the heck are you doing in there, pup?

C'mon, you better get out now and head home."

He requested, pleaded, admonished and ordered, but the animal continued to stay in place, flashing him a doggy smile and looking like he had every right to be there.

Then it occurred to him, "Of course you don't speak, I mean, understand English."

Alex looked around and there wasn't a house in sight.

"Move over, pup. I guess you just got yourself a chauffeur. Let's see if we can find where you live."

Alex pulled into the first service station and made some inquiries, but no one recognized the dog. They assured him that no one in the area kept dogs like that.

The attendant at the third station he pulled into shed some light on the situation. "Da trucker, you know, day keep dog, how you say? for da company—dat's dis dog and den, he might get tired of him or da dog jump out."

Back in his truck, Alex patted the tin of ashes. "Well, Gramps, it looks like we've got ourselves some company until I find a home for this fellow. No sense looking around here any more."

And to the dog: "Whoa, buddy! Slow down! You just inhaled a-bout seven dollars' worth of beef jerky. I better find us a grocery store and get you some proper dog food before you bankrupt me."

Alex made a point of pulling off the highway near residential areas and letting the dog out to relieve itself. His theory was that if the dog decided to pull a

Littlest Hobo routine and wander off, he would probably find himself a decent home far better than the old truck. But, to his disappointment, the dog showed no inclination to stray and the moment he opened the truck door, the animal barged passed him and reclaimed his seat.

It was during one of these layovers that Alex discovered that the dog had been deceiving him.

Alex had been passing the time between stops trying to call on his high-school French for commands that the dog might understand, but he wasn't having much luck. Whenever he tried saying 's'asseoir' or 'rester' the dog would just stare at him with a perplexed look on his face.

"I must not be pronouncing this correctly."

The truth of the matter became apparent during a stop outside the town of Amherst in Nova Scotia. Without thinking, Alex said, 'Sit' instead of 's'asseoir' and the dog sat.

So he tried 'Lie down' and the dog dropped onto his stomach. Noticeably annoyed now, Alex shouted 'Heel' and the dog followed him over to a nearby stream. Alex watched, miffed while the Shepherd slurped away.

"You dirty little scoundrel. You've been putting me on. You understood everything I said to you when you invaded my truck; you just had no intention of leaving. Well, try this, 'Sit'. Now 'Stay!'"

At that Alex turned away and marched over to the truck and opened the door, fully expecting the dog to race past him and leap into the truck. But when he turned around to check, the dog was still sitting in place looking sad and dejected. Even when he climbed into the truck and started the motor, the dog remained in place.

It was when he rolled down the window and heard the dog whining that he lost heart, climbed out of the truck and called for him to come.

The dog was over in flash, and tail wagging, he reared up and placed his feet on Alex's chest and tried to lick his face.

"Get down, you brute! You're not getting off that easy. Now sit! Now roll over!."

The dog was quick to comply and was rewarded by some rough petting and a reluctant invitation back into the truck.

"I guess I'm stuck with you for a while, so I better give you a temporary name. My granddad's dog was called Jack and you look a lot like him, so for now I'll call you 'Jack'. But don't get too used to it, because I'm going get rid of you as soon as I can."

Leaning over, Alex opened the passenger-side window just enough so that Jack could travel with a portion of his muzzle out to catch the wind.

14: Tattoos

After he gassed up at a service station outside Truro, Alex got directions to the RCMP detachment. Considering Jack's appearance and his now obvious degree of training he might well be a police dog.

Great: I maybe just crossed a provincial border with what will appear to be stolen police property. We're going to clear this up right away.

Alex took a couple of wrong turns that had him doing a tour of the town before he found the police station. He was struck by the many large carved wooden statues he passed. Later he learned that they were ghosts carved out of the mighty elms that once shaded the streets.

His inquiry at the police station didn't take long. The desk sergeant said that there were no reports of AWOL RCMP dogs on the wire and, for that matter, no reports of any other missing German Shepherd dogs.

To be doubly sure the sergeant agreed to come out and examine the dog. Jack sat quietly on the truck seat while the Mountie examined each ear, the gum under his lip and the inside of each thigh.

"No tattoos; you're good to go."

Alex found the Feeds'n Needs store and bought a large bag of dry dog food, a feed bowl, a water dish, a good collar and a leash. Then for better or for worse, the unlikely couple set off on the last leg of the journey to their destination.

15: All original

Alex shoved Jack aside, rolled out of bed, noted the time on the clock radio and then headed for the bathroom, adjusting his watch to Atlantic Time. The Middleton Motel, while other similar businesses were shutting down because of the competition from the more modern motel/hotels around Kentville area, was still flourishing. Staying there with its gaudy rugs, mass-produced prints, laminated particle-board furniture and mandatory Gideon bible in the beside table was like a trip back into the nineteen fifties.

He was hungry and not even the caustic aroma of recently-applied insecticide was quelling his appetite. It didn't bother the dog, either. After wetting his whistle in the toilet bowl, Jack plunged muzzle deep into a bowl of his new, expensive, dry dog food.

Looking down at him, Alex said, "You amuse yourself, greedy guts. I'm off to find some grub for myself."

The nearby diner was close to full of truckers and salesmen, but there was one lone table available near the cashier. Alex seated himself there and flipped over the coffee-stained menu card.

A fortyish waitress with dyed blonde hair and a liberal coating of lipstick and blue eye shadow finished running a gauntlet of gropers and presented herself, pen and paper in hand, in front of his table. "What'll it be this morning, skipper?"

"That special looks good. I think I'll try that and a pot of tea."

"How do you want your eggs—not that it makes any difference. The cook's going to send you whatever's sitting on the grill anyway. I'll bring your tea right along. Would you like your bag squeezed?"

At that, the men at the table next to him broke out in laughter. It was obvious that it was not the first time that she had offered this special service.

When the waitress returned with his meal, he detained her for a moment to ask for directions.

She had no idea where Spa Springs was, but the old cashier who was in earshot leaned over the counter. "Finish your meal, then come over and I'll tell you how to get there."

Alex ate his meal slowly, left a hefty tip on the table and then went up to the cashier.

"You head north on Commercial Street until you hit the intersection with Highway 362, then turn right for a couple of miles and watch on your left, just before a road that heads north over the mountain. Better watch close, cuz there ain't much to see. I can draw you a map if you want."

"No, that's okay, thanks, I think I'll be able to find it." Alex made a mental note to extend his stay at the motel for another night.

On his way back toward his room, Alex noticed a half dozen or so of the men he had been sharing breakfast with gathered around his truck.

"Is that yours?" a man who had been at the table to next to him asked.

"Yeah, it used to be my grandfather's but it's mine now."

"You've done a hell of a job restoring it "

"No, it's all original. My grandfather bought it new in 1948 and, other than a couple of short trips to keep it in shape, it's been in a garage its whole life. My trip from Toronto has put more miles on it than it had in all the time my grandfather owned it."

"That's an International KB1, isn't it? The Reagh Brothers in town here used to sell them. They're a great old rig. I don't suppose you'd like to sell it."

"No can do—my grandfather would roll over in his grave."

It wasn't really a legitimate response because Dan Johnson wasn't in his grave. Most of his ashes were still in the glove box of the truck.

16: Private property

Alex let Jack out of the room and threw his gear in the truck while the dog headed over to the nearest tree and lifted his leg. Then he opened the driver's side door and the dog jumped in and seated himself in the passenger seat.

Alex started the engine and headed the old truck east on Route 1 to the centre of town, then swung north where two banks, like sentinels of commerce, sat on either corner of the beginning of Commercial Street. After a quick trip through the typical small town retail section and a short jaunt past open fields, the sign directing him to Spa Springs appeared. He would have to drive more slowly now. The motel clerk had been right.

There wasn't much to see and he was already abreast of a gravel road that headed up the mountain when he realized that he had come a little too far.

He decided to pull over and walk back for a closer look. Jack ranged back and forth, keeping pace with Alex while collecting all the news his nose could handle.

When he heard the sound of a brook passing through a culvert under him, Alex stopped. A stand of mature hardwoods met the ditch on the north side of the highway. The spring that his grandfather had mentioned must be hidden somewhere among them.

He turned and headed back to the truck. If his grandfather's instructions were correct, and if they still were there, the old house and blacksmith shop should be just a couple of miles further along.

While Jack settled himself again, Alex dug the framed photo out of his rucksack and placed it leaning against the dog. "Here goes, Gramps."

Focusing his attention on the north side of the paved road, he ambled along in second gear. He passed several newly-built houses on the south side before the building came into view.

Sitting almost on the highway, where another rough woods road wound its way up the mountain, a dilapidated building displayed rusty metal signs boasting that it had once been a garage.

Alex hoped that he was wrong, but when he picked up the photo and compared it to what was confronting him, there was no doubt. He couldn't help himself and began to cry. "Dear god, Gramps, I'm sorry. I'm so sorry."

The blacksmith shop that stood solidly and square in the photo was now swaybacked and tilting dangerously from the windward. There was no trace of the grand old house and woodshed that appeared in the photo. In their place was an expansive collection of rusting cars and discarded washing machines.

Only a dried-up skeleton of the stately elm in the photo remained. It stood naked but for a series of tin signs advertising motor oil and soft drinks that had been tacked onto it.

"The place looks deserted, Jack. Maybe if I have a closer look there might be something worth finding. Something, anything still there from the day that picture was taken. Come on, dog."

Alex opened the truck door, stepped onto the running board and was about to let Jack out when a snarling Doberman Pinscher exploded out of his hiding place and came charging directly at him. He just managed to fall back into the truck with Jack snarling and trying to climb over him to get at the strange dog.

He pulled the door closed just as the heavy chain that was trailing behind the dog reached it maximum length and the sudden stop flipped the animal off his legs and onto his back.

The dog squirmed back onto his feet and tightened his chain enough to allow him to plant his paws on the running board, still snarling, blowing drool and snot on the window.

Jack was barking frantically and trying to get past Alex. "Get back to your seat, you crazy bastard! That dog could eat you."

Alex elbowed the dog aside and fumbled to start the truck and find first gear. He was just about to disengage the clutch when the Doberman suddenly flew backwards toward the building.

A tall, grey-haired man in bib overalls and a plaid

shirt was reeling the dog back toward him, cursing with each haul on the chain.

When he had the dog close enough he gave it two sound kicks in the stomach. "Get the hell back to your barrel, you no good son of a bitch."

As the dog moved off whining, with his tail between his legs, Alex rolled his window down and spoke.

"I'm sorry. I didn't mean to upset your dog."

The man spat a dark stream of tobacco juice. "What the hell do you think you're doing anyway?" He pointed a thumb back over his shoulder. "That sign says private property. No trespassing. My dog could have ripped your balls off. That's why I keep him around. I don't like strangers poking around my place."

"I guess I pulled into the wrong place. I was looking for somebody else."

Another spit, then, "Who was you looking for?"

Without knowing why he was saying it, Alex replied, "I'm looking for Dan Johnson."

"There ain't no Dan Johnson around here, so you better just git."

As Alex made his way back toward Middleton, he thought about what he had said to the man. In a sense he was looking for Dan Johnson; maybe not *where* he was but *who* he was.

17: Not so very new anymore

As Alex reached the spot where he had been told to look for signs of the spring, he slowly passed a parked Volkswagen campervan decorated in a gaudy flower pattern. Several young men and women were heading into the woods with a variety of plastic water jugs in their hands. When they saw him, they all turned and flashed the peace symbol.

Alex spent the rest of the morning touring Middleton. His grandfather had only provided a very scant picture of what life had been like for him before he joined the army and shipped off, never to return. He once spoke of a fairly new Armoury where he had signed up. A plate in the gable of the building read 1903.

"Not so very new any more," he said to Jack, who cocked his ear, trying hard to understand.

He turned left by the town hall and hadn't gone very far when, to his left, a huge red building appeared. "Looks like your old alma mater is still there, Gramps."

As he cruised Commercial Street for a second look, many of the stores appeared old enough to have been there in his grandfather's time.

He had a quick lunch at Eisner's Restaurant and then headed back to the motel to retrieve his briefcase.

Tomorrow he would have to do some exploring of the property he had inherited and he wanted to clarify its validity. The only copy of the deed he had was a photocopy of an ancient document written in barely-legible cursive. The lawyer in Toronto assured him that the deed had been transferred into his name and properly recorded in the Annapolis County Registry Office, but Alex wanted an up-to-date copy with his name on it in his hand before attempting to find the property and establish its boundaries.

18: Easy-peasy

"Just stay on Highway One, head west and follow your nose—you can't go wrong," the man seated at the table next to Alex's at Eisnor's had explained. "That's the oldest courthouse and registry office still operating in Canada. You can't miss it: it's on a rise over the Basin next to Fort Anne and the old Garrison Burial Ground. You should have a good look around while you're there; lots of history, lots of history."

Alex had thanked the man, but knew he wouldn't be spending much time in the old town. He was on a mission and time was of the essence.

He jumped into the truck, gave Jack the T-bone he had saved from his dinner to apologize for leaving him stuck in the truck for so long, and off they went.

The old road followed the Annapolis River as it snaked its way along the base of the Valley, passing through several towns—Lawrencetown, Paradise, and Bridgetown. Then there was a string of Granvilles (Upper, Middle, and Ferry), and then the road swung across the river and into Annapolis Royal.

The courthouse was easy to find; the man at the restaurant had described it well.

He parked the truck, wound the windows half way down, and made his way into the old building. The first person he met directed Alex to the lower level, where the Registry Office was located.

A man in his late fifties, dressed in a white shirt and a loose tie, emerged from behind an office divider and removed his reading glasses. "How can I help you?"

Alex lifted his briefcase onto the counter and dug out the papers he wanted. He sifted through several pages, found what he was looking for, and then proffered the old deed for the man behind the counter to inspect.

"I want to make sure that this is valid and in order."

"Let me see…let me see," the man mouthed as he drew in closer and replaced his glasses for a closer look.

"Yup…yup. You might be in luck. There's a whole crew digitizing the records in all those dusty old files in the next room, but I think this year might be already on the computer. Let me check."

The man disappeared into a cubicle and emerged a few minutes later with good news. "Still seems like magic to me, but it's there and everything is in order. It also shows that all the taxes are up to date and the current assessment has been issued. I'm printing you off another copy of the deed but I have to charge you two dollars."

"Thank you very much. That eases my mind, but I still have to figure out just where the land is situated."

"Easy-peasy. Just follow me"

The clerk came from behind the counter and went directly to a computer stationed by the wall. He attacked the keyboard with a practised flourish of his fingers.

"This is called Property on Line, and that square right there shows where your property is. I can print you off a copy of this, too, but it will cost you another two dollars."

"Hit the print button, man: that's great."

As the printer whirred, Alex said, "Maybe you can help me with something else. My deed states that I have a right of way over the property with the blacksmith shop on it. It may be my only access, but I'm not comfortable approaching the owner for permission to use it."

"I've lived in Middleton my whole life, but I don't know of any blacksmith shop up that way."

"I guess it looks more like a poor excuse for a garage now."

"Homer Leonard's place? You'd best give that fella a wide berth. Anyway, I know that area, used to hunt rabbits up that way. The property south of yours was clear-cut a few years ago, probably cut right to your boundary line, and I know there's a good woods road into it. I think I'd be getting to your property that way. Everybody around there knows that Leonard is bad news."

"Just one more thing: can you tell from that chart where the old cemetery is located?"

"Cemetery? I've never heard of any cemetery up that way."

19: A white marker stake

Alex sat in his truck, parked in front of his motel unit, studying the 'Property Online' chart he had acquired from the Registry Office, comparing it to the scanty information on his road map. *Obviously an older map—no woods road shown on here.*

If the road was where the county clerk had told him it was, Alex would have to drive past the old blacksmith shop, take the next road north to the brow of the mountain and watch for signs of it.

Earlier, while ordering his breakfast he'd added a bagged lunch to go and his thermos filled with tea. "And please don't bother to squeeze my bag this morning, Hon!"

"Got it, skipper—but just this once."

He started the truck and, while he waited the mandatory time that his grandfather insisted that it needed to warm up, went over a checklist of the things he might need for the day. It didn't look like it was going to rain, but he remembered what the waitress had said when he'd asked her if she'd heard the forecast that morning: "If you don't like the weather in Nova Scotia, just wait an hour or so."

A yellow rain jacket and the pair of heavy-duty

rubber boots that he had purchased at Canadian Tire a few miles down the road in Greenwood sat, off-gassing, on the floor on the passenger side; and a new hatchet, compass and roll of bright plastic marking tape sat beside the tobacco can on the seat. Jack, sporting his newly-purchased and stronger collar, was crowded over close to the passenger window.

Alex was wearing a pair of blue jeans, a plaid shirt and an old pair of his grandfather's police-issue, lace-up beat boots. They fit perfectly and the liberal coating of Dubbin he'd worked into them had softened them and taken away the squeaks.

"I guess that's all I'll need for now."

The metal trunk in the back of the truck was the one his grandfather used to hold the tools he had needed to moved between his house and his cottage annually. It had an assortment of everything that Alex figured might come in handy.

He wasn't looking forward to passing the old home place again, but it was on the shortest route to where he wanted to be.

The speed limit was 50 km/h in that vicinity, and he kept to the maximum. As he drove by the black-smith's shop, he stole a glance. The place looked deserted. No sign of the man he now knew as Homer Leonard, or his dog.

Alex could see the signs for the road he was looking for looming into view, so he geared down, applied the brakes and turned left off the pavement and headed up the mountain.

It was a well-maintained gravel road that, he was glad to find, was wide enough for him to give way to a huge fully loaded log truck that came barrelling down the mountain in the opposite direction scant seconds after he began his assent.

As he reached what appeared to be the top of the mountain, he was greeted by the moonscape of a total clear-cut as far as the eye could see. A small fire road running at right angles to the one he was on seemed to be declaring a boundary between the sad, despoiled-looking land to the north and a tall, verdant, untouched old-growth forest standing steadfast to the south.

"This must it. I hope there's somewhere to turn around if I'm wrong."

He kept the truck in first gear, plodding along as he searched for something, but not exactly sure what it was or where it would be.

It was slow going, to say the least. He had to stop frequently and climb out of the truck for a closer look, but eventually he spotted a huge spruce tree on the south side of the road hung with long strips of differently-coloured marking tape. Nestled beneath the tree was a white marker stake surrounded by stones.

Alex made a note of the numbers etched on the Crown Marker, then headed back to the truck to consult his property plan.

Well, what do you know? These numbers match. Welcome home, Gramps! This is the northwest corner of your property.

Let me see: the deed says this property is fifty-two rods wide. This chart says that a rod is 16.5 feet or 5.5 yards. If my pace is three feet that means that…can that be right: 286 paces? I guess that's right, Gramps, so I'll give it a try.

Alex, with Jack on his leash, set off, restraining the urge to lengthen his strides as he passed what he thought was half way to his goal. He needn't have worried, because long before he finished counting he could see in the distance the other Crown Marker that fixed the northeast corner of the property.

As he made his way back to the truck, Alex couldn't believe his luck. It had been too easy. "Just over an hour and we've already established the northern boundary of the property, Jack."

20: Are you all right, brother?

Alex had been focusing his attention on the south side of the road as he counted his way in, so he hadn't noticed the big, cleared turnaround area on the northern, clear-cut, side of the road.

Too easy—it just gets better. I'll be in and out of here in flash.

It was after he had driven forward, swung around, and pointed the truck back toward the main road that he noticed it. A passing cloud parted and the sun exposed something partially hidden in the brush skirting the trees on the south side of the road. On his land.

"What are you doing here, little fella? C'mon, Jack, let's have a look."

He shut the truck off and walked over for a closer look.

A five-foot-high Inuksuk stood there, with its stone arms spread wide in a welcoming gesture. But most interesting was the shaded path that led off into the woods behind it.

"I wonder who has gone to the trouble to create such an elaborate marker. And where does the path go, and what could it be for? Probably hunters—

hunters on my property without permission!"

Jack didn't seem to have any answers for him.

When it occurred to Alex that there were no 'No Hunting' signs posted and that people had probably been hunting on the land without objection for a hundred years or more, his possessive snit abated and he headed back to the truck to gather his gear.

He strapped on the belt that held his hunting knife and sheathed hatchet, checked his pockets for his compass and cell phone, and then slung the leather backpack that contained his lunch, water bottle and thermos of tea onto his back. He took up Jack's leash and they headed out once again, set for a good explore.

Alex patted the stone that served as the Inuksuk's head, and they struck off down the path with Jack hunting and sniffing along incessantly. No need to use the marking ribbon. The path was well-worn and marked by periodic blazes. There was no sign of the tree stands for hunters that he assumed he would be seeing.

The deed said that the property was 328 rods deep. *That's over a mile as the crow flies*. He could have calculated how many steps that would involve, but the trail was winding, often turning back on itself before continuing in a southerly direction, so there would be no point.

He had no idea where the old cemetery would be. Since his grandfather had spoken of it being somewhere above the home place, he assumed that he would find it, if he ever did, closer to the southern boundary than the northern.

He hadn't been walking for long when the dense, dark cover of old spruce and fir gave way to a mixed stand of hardwoods: maple, birch, ash and poplar interspersed with huge lone pines and hemlocks, a true Acadian forest like the ones his grandfather had told him about logging in his teenage years. The going became more difficult as he cautiously made his way over a series of rock ledges. Finding the site of the graveyard was not going to be easy.

Alex had stumbled on an article about the shameful condition of abandoned cemeteries in the province and was prepared for the worst. If he was able to find some small sign of its presence, he would at least be able to spread his grandfather's ashes there. *It probably won't be in the kind of place you imagined it would be, Gramps, but if it's possible, I'll get you there.*

As he moved along, a series of clouds passed over and he thought about his rain jacket back in the car. *Not much use to me back there.*

A few yards further on, a small but active brook crossed the path at the base of a huge rock promontory. The big rock sloped upwards and only a few tree tops were visible beyond where it seemed to end against the sky.

The top of that will make a great vantage point.

There was still that brook to cross. Someone had arranged stepping stones, but they were partially submerged...and his rubber boots were also sitting useless, beside his rain jacket, in the truck.

Alex pulled off his boots and socks, rolled up his pants legs and, cradling his boots in his arms, braved the icy water.

As he stepped carefully from the final slippery flat rock to the security of a huge granite slab, he decided to walk barefoot to the overhang at the summit, a good place to sit down and get his socks and army boots back on.

When he reached the top, an incredible vista opened up; he was looking down over a patchwork of small farms nestled along the Annapolis River. He could see the roof of the blacksmith shop, surrounded by the rusting vehicles and appliances.

But when he dropped his vision down and beyond his bare feet to the base of the cliff, he saw something that made him gasp in wonder. In a large meadow at the base of the rock, three tombstones sat reflecting the light from an afternoon sun that had just broken through the clouds.

Dear god! Is that possible? Am I seeing things? Did I stray off the property? That must be someone else's graveyard.

But Alex wasn't dreaming. When he and Jack finally struggled down off the ledge and examined the monuments closely, it was a miracle confirmed. Time had taken its toll on the old stones, but the carved names were still legible. The discoloration on the faces of the stone suggested that they had lain partially buried for a long time, and that someone had recently returned them to their proper posture and cleaned them up, even though they seemed to be riddled and chipped with what appeared to be bullet scars.

Some damned hunters must have used them for target practice.

The area around the grave markers was neat and tidy, with wild grass growing among the hundreds of closely-cut stumps of alder bushes that must have concealed the site. They seemed freshly sheared.

Small bunches of wild flowers lay on the graves —"ditch flowers" was how the waitress had described them when one of her customers mockingly presented her with a bouquet at breakfast. But they seemed beautiful and appropriate here.

It was the sight of those flowers that brought it on: an overwhelming feeling of sadness seized him and, leaning on the closest marker, he began to sob.

He'd been fixed at the same spot for a long time, head down, trying to regain his composure when Jack started to growl and a voice out of nowhere startled him.

"Are you all right, brother? This is a special place and it had our whole family crying the same way when we first found it. You're a couple of days early, but that's good. C'mon, follow me and meet the rest of the folks. I'm Saul Levy, but of course you already know that."

Saul, a man somewhere around Alex's age but shorter and slightly built, with a huge crop of blond hair under a knitted multi-coloured yamaka, stood at the entrance of a different path from the one Alex had arrived on, beckoning for him to follow.

Alex might have spoken up and clarified the situation, but curiosity had the better of him. He had to know who these apparently-benign trespassers were and why they, strangers, had gone to so much trouble to restore his family's place of rest.

"You can let your dog off the leash, if you want," Saul said.

He led the way, periodically glancing back and addressing Alex as if he knew who he was and why he was there. "The folks at Johnson's Commune said you'd be along as soon as you got up from Halifax. I'm sure the sisters will be pleased when they see you."

Sisters? Commune? What the hell is he talking about?

Shortly they arrived at a sizable open meadow. A large, military-type tent dominated the scene, but several smaller tents were scattered around its perimeter. Jack had made it to the campsite well ahead of the men and was already enjoying the attention of four women seated around an open fire.

"Ladies, I want you to meet our guest—Jesus, I didn't even get your name."

"Alex...my name is Alex but...I don't know your names, either."

"Of course, how stupid of me. I just assumed that you had been briefed about us over in Harmony. Gather around, ladies, and I'll make the introductions."

Two identical-looking, blonde young women, dressed in similar tie dyed moo moos, stepped forward.

"Alex, meet Dawn and Heather. I know, it's hard to tell them apart. I have trouble myself sometimes, but it really doesn't matter since they're both my wives."

Alex took a step backward in shock but remained silent.

"This is my other wife, Marina," Saul continued. "We've been married for, well, it seems like forever, doesn't it, Marina?"

Marina, a tall, olive-skinned, wispy beauty with shiny black hair, gathered her long skirt and moved over to join the twins, while a fourth woman, who was holding a child on her hip, remained in the background, watching.

"Come on over and say hello to Alex, Nancy...No? Well, okay. Nancy is a guest here. We like to think of her as part of the family. Is that tea in the pot? C'mon, Alex, grab a seat and join us."

Even at a distance Alex could see that there was something different, aloof and special about the woman, like a blonde, blue-eyed Madonna, holding the child. She reminded him of the private-school girls back in Toronto.

The three 'wives' found seats on the logs that served as benches around the fire pit. Alex took a seat and accepted a tin mug of herbal tea while Saul continued to hold court.

21: I should pinch myself

"I think we should get right down to business, Alex," Saul said. "These girls have been living together for so long that their monthlies have coincided, so they all should be ovulating at the same time next week or so. Is that right, Marina?"

Marina looked at the twins for confirmation. Then they all nodded in agreement.

"So, Alex, there's no time to waste. You've got to get on with it."

Alex jumped to his feet, spilling the hot amber liquid on his jeans. "Get on with what? What the hell are you talking about?"

"Easy now. I know we're all anxious and a bit afraid—after all, this is a wonderful thing we are all embarking on. But there is no one here more responsible and involved than me in what we are about to do, and I'm thankful for your part in it. I assume you have been told why it has become necessary? No? Well, let me explain. There is poem by Leigh Hunt that you might be familiar with..."

"'Abou Ben Adhem (may his tribe increase!)'?"

"That's it, Alex. That poem has been taunting this family. We've all been yearning for our tribe to increase. But it wasn't happening, and it finally dawned on me that, since three wives and the occasional visitor weren't getting pregnant despite my efforts, that the fault might lie with me. I decided to consult a doctor. He took one look at my package then asked me if I had ever had the mumps. He said I ought to have a sperm test just to be sure. Well, it turns out that I've been shooting blanks. I'm not ashamed, but that's why we need your services."

Before Alex could react, Saul jumped to his feet, pulled down his sweat pants and exposed himself. "I ask you: is this anything to be ashamed of?"

Alex wasn't sure how to reply, but the women seemed to be waiting for his answer. He gave the appendage a quick, glancing appraisal and ventured a guarded opinion. "Ah, everything seems to be in order down there, Saul."

The three wives broke into smiles.

With that matter put to rest, Alex thought a quick exit might be in order. "I've got some business to take care of this afternoon, so, if you don't mind, I'll take off for now and join you folks again tomorrow. Come along, Jack."

"Great! We're planning a sunrise ceremony tomorrow, and you don't want to miss it."

Saul showed Alex and the dog the shorter, more direct route back to the fire road and walked with them, chatting away, until they arrived at the turnaround where the truck was, with the Volkswagen van that Alex had seen down by Spa Spring parked beside it.

He opened the truck door, shooed Jack in and climbed in after him. Starting the engine, he looked around nervously before popping the clutch and gunned the truck, spraying gravel all the way to the main road. He felt that he had just witnessed a scene from *One Flew over the Cuckoo's Nest* and he wanted to be out of there and on his way back to the motel as fast as possible.

Maybe I should pinch myself to see if I'm awake. I can't believe that really happened—or, for that matter, what the hell I'm going to do about it. Should I call the police? They're trespassing and they sure as hell are wackos. What the hell is that Saul smoking? Gramps, are you there? Any chance of you sending me some kind of a sign or something?

22: I don't know what you're up to

Alex swooshed the old truck into the parking spot in front of his unit at the motel, turned Jack loose, hurried inside and plopped down on the bed. He lay back and watched the progress a spider was making on the ceiling above him while he went over the events of the day.

When he got to the part where Saul made his appearance he thought a dose of some sanity and bit of dinner were in order. Jack had been scratching at the door, so he made sure the dog's food and water bowls were full before he let him in and went out himself, closing the door behind him.

The restaurant was nearly full, but there was one spot close to the big round table where a group of the obviously-retired men from the community spent most of their time.

When the waitress approached him, wielding her yellow chit pad, Alex chose the food he wanted and then placed a side order for some of her homespun wisdom.

"Tell me, Martha—it is Martha, isn't it?—I've been learning a bit about some of the things going on in communes around here. I need an opinion. How do you feel about all these so-called group relationships?"

Martha thought for while, then replied, "I don't know what you're up to, Sonny, but as long as the other girls you've got lined up are easy to get along with, I'm in!"

The old boys at the next table broke out into raucous laughter and watched as she drifted off in the direction of the kitchen, playfully accentuating the sway of her ample bottom.

When the laughter died down, the man seated closest to Alex spun his chair around and said, "I've been wondering about them communes myself. God knows there's quite a few of them in the Valley now, mostly up on North Mountain. But I happened on one on South Mountain when I was up hunting there last fall. They'd built themselves an A-frame house, but when I happened on them, they was all outside enjoying the sun, roaming around stark naked!"

As was the custom at the round table, once a subject was broached, it was open for discussion, debate and the sharing of opinions. A second man added, "You ought to see the kind of houses they're building. It's not that I'm nosy, but up on the North Mountain alone, I've seen people shacked up in lean-tos, tepees, and treehouses. There's even a few of them things they call domes. It makes you wonder what the world is coming to."

23: The sunrise ceremony

"Jesus, Jack, they didn't give us the wakeup call. What's the point of offering a service if they don't follow through? Damn! We're already late, so let's get a move on!"

The German Shepherd jumped down off the bed and Alex threw off the covers and hit the floor, searching for his clothes and boots. A quick zip and a tuck and a look around to make sure all the stuff they had was packed in anticipation of the early morning start, and they were off. The dog beat him to the truck and leapt in as soon as Alex opened the door.

They sped off through town, passed the spring and the blacksmith shop and bounced on up the mountain. When his headlights revealed the parked Volkswagen van, Alex saw a green Austin Mini sitting alongside it. He pulled the old truck in beside them, grabbed his backpack and flashlight, and he and Jack headed down the path into the woods.

A huge fire illuminated the clearing, but no one seemed to be there. As they drew closer Jack started to bark and went running toward a pup tent situated further back from the circle of improvised enclosures.

Alex hurried forward and caught up with Jack, who had suddenly stopped barking and had come to a halt at the entrance to the little tent. He was staring intently, his head in the tent, his tail wagging.

Nancy, the woman who had drawn Alex's attention the day before, was busy changing a diaper on her little boy. Unperturbed, she looked up and said, "Good morning, Alex. I'm a little surprised to see you here today. "

"Yes, Nancy. It is Nancy, isn't it? I guess I should have explained things yesterday but I kind of got caught off-guard and didn't know what to say. But I'd like to straighten things out now. Where are the rest of the folks?"

"You've just missed them—they're down at the cemetery to begin the ceremony."

"At the cemetery! Why at the cemetery?"

"It's their sacred place, Alex. It's why they chose to live here."

"They? Not 'we'? Aren't you all part of the family?"

"Goodness no! I'm just visiting. I respect and love them all but I'm not part of their movement. I think the things that they do like the Sunrise Ceremony are wonderful, and I like to watch their rituals, but I don't take part. I'm going over to watch them now. Would you like to join me?"

Nancy crawled out of the tent, stood up, balanced her son on her hip and led the way.

They were headed to the big rock that overlooked the graveyard. They had only gone a short distance when she stopped, turned around and said, "I should warn you that Horst, the man everybody mistook you for yesterday, showed up last evening. He's taking part in the ceremony this morning."

"Great! Thanks for the heads-up." *Can this thing get more fucked up?*

By the time they reached their destination, Alex no longer needed his flashlight. The sun was just making its way over the horizon. As they made their way close to the edge of the precipice, the sound of a low murmuring chant intensified.

A man, a woman, her child and a curious German Shepherd stood watching while below three women and two men, all completely naked, stood in a half-circle holding hands, staring at the sunrise.

Alex looked askance at Nancy.

"It's what they do. Do you like the incantation? Saul wrote it."

"It's okay, I guess. The lyrics are good but the melody sounds like something I remember from *Jesus Christ Superstar.*" *Why did I say that?* "Sorry, I didn't mean to make fun. As soon as they are through with their ceremony, I'm going to get everything straightened out with everybody."

They watched as the group below finished singing and began a series of ritual embraces, after which it became apparent that Horst, Alex's replacement, was definitely up for the task ahead.

24: The reveal

Alex lent a hand stirring up the dying embers of the fire and swinging the large cast-iron pot full of water into place while Nancy fussed about preparing the food for the communal breakfast. It would be lots of fruits and vegetables, washed down by the coffee they would make by simply tossing the grounds into the boiling water.

He couldn't help speculating that Horst was going to need a diet with a lot more protein, what with the demands of his assignment.

Oh shit, here they come and they're still in the buff.

Saul led the pack, with Horst trotting behind him, followed by the gaggle of excited women. As soon as Saul spied Alex, he ran over and enveloped him in a sweaty embrace that lasted way too long and then broke free to usher him over to a seat by the fire.

"Alex, let me introduce you to my friend and assistant, Horst Anderson."

Horst swung his arms wide and made to advance at Alex for a hug, but pudgy Heather intercepted him. She grabbed his arm and dragged him off in the direction of her tent.

Horst yelled back a quick apology. "I'll be back shortly. We can get acquainted then!"

He was as good as his word, and by the time the coffee was ready he was back and eager for some less physical intercourse.

A proud Saul slapped him on the back. "That's my boy. You're doing a great job. Isn't he doing a great job, Alex? By the way, Alex if you're so inclined, none of us would be averse to you contributing to our little gene bank."

Alex shot a frantic look over at Nancy, then mumbled, "Don't get me wrong. I'm honoured but I don't think I...I mean I don't think it would be...you know, cool. That's it. It wouldn't be cool."

Christ, cool, give me a break. Where on earth did that come from?

When he looked over, Nancy was smirking at him.

"Anyway, while you're all here, I want to explain myself."

At that they all grabbed their coffee cups and drew into a tight circle around Alex. Jack abandoned a stick he was chewing and came over to lie down at his feet.

"The reason I came here yesterday was to fulfill a promise I made to a very special person. He told me about the graveyard up here and asked me to spread his ashes among the graves. I came all the way from Toronto to follow his wishes. I didn't expect to find you folks here but," he stole a glance at Nancy, "I'm really glad that you're here and that you've been looking after the place the way you have. I'm wondering if you folks would mind if I spread his ashes. I won't trouble you further, since I have to get back to Toronto shortly. I've got commitments there."

When he looked over at Saul, the man had tears in his eyes.

"That is so fucking beautiful, man." He turned to the others, "Isn't that the most beautiful fucking thing you ever heard? Of course you can spread those ashes. One more beautiful spirit among the ones already there. We can help. Maybe we can have a special ceremony like the one we had this morning."

"Oh. I don't know what Gramps…"

"What was that?"

"Nothing, it was nothing. Great idea—I'm in!"

Saul led the drawing up of plans for the following day and Alex and Jack took their leave.

25: A can of Dan

Maybe Alex should have stayed longer that afternoon and come clean about whose ashes he wanted scattered on the old graveyard, but he chose not to. If he had, he knew he would have been tied up for hours explaining himself and his relationship to the land the commune was on, and there were other things he needed to do.

After seeing the cemetery he decided that he would like to bury the small tin of his grandfather's ashes between his mother and father's graves, rather than scattering them. If he had had time, he would have purchased a fancy urn big enough to hold the tobacco can, but he didn't really have the time, and anyway, considering how humble and unassuming his Gramps could be on his good days, the rusty old can seemed appropriate somehow.

He was able to order and pay for a simple flat granite marker, but it would be several days before it could be engraved and delivered from Windsor, at the eastern end of the Valley. So now his idea of a quick departure seemed to be disappearing, unless he could arrange something with Saul.

Why, he wondered, *now that I probably have to*

stay the extra time, am I thinking about how Nancy and her baby looked on that first day?

The next morning, as arranged, Alex waited with Nancy and Jimmy on the rock ledge above the little graveyard while the rest of the family performed a sort of a sweet grass purification of the area. Then Saul looked up to him and indicated that it was time for him to deliver his eulogy.

He helped Nancy and Jimmy down the narrow pathway that wound around the side of the outcropping. Leaving the mother and child a discrete distance from the others, he took his place between the two Johnson graves.

He and Nancy were the only two present who were clothed, but the others' nudity didn't seem to take anything away from the solemnity of the occasion. Besides, he knew if his grandfather was looking down from above or out from his tobacco can, as the case might be, he would get a kick out of the situation.

Resting his hand on the can, he said, "The man whose ashes are in this can would not be pleased with me. He taught me never to lie and that withholding the truth amounts to the same thing. So, I should have said what I'm about to say when we first met. I kept it to myself and I'm not sure why."

He had everyone's attention.

"The man in the can's name is Dan Johnson, my grandfather. Johnson, the same name as the one on this tombstone. That Johnson was my grandfather's father—my great grandfather."

He turned to touch the stone beside it, and said, "And this is his mother, my great grandmother, Lily Johnson. If you look down the slope you can make out the old garage by the road. It was once a blacksmith shop, with a house and barn. That's where my grandfather was born and lived until he joined the army during World War I. That other stone is where my great grandfather's best friend is buried."

Alex remained silent for several seconds before continuing, "I'm really sorry to spring this on you. I should have handled it differently. Are you still okay with this? Can we go ahead with the ceremony?"

Saul enveloped Alex in another sweaty embrace, while tears ran down his face. "This just keeps getting fucking better and better. I knew these folks buried here were trying to tell us something. Didn't I say that, Horst? Didn't I say that? This is wonderful. Can we spread the ashes now?"

"Well, I sort of changed my mind on that one, Saul. I think I'd like to bury my grandfather's ashes between his parents."

"Too right! I'll get a shovel, man."

The interment went on with great ceremony. Then everybody returned to the campsite and gathered around the fire pit. They fired questions at Alex from every direction, and he answered them as best he could. But he still had one important secret that he was reluctant to tell.

26: Jolly Jumper

Waiting for the marker was going to delay things, but eventually Alex would have to head back to Toronto. The big city was no place for a dog like Jack and, besides, Alex had never meant to keep him.

He played with the idea of stopping near the spot where he had found the dog, or, more correctly, where the dog had found him, but that was too chancy; better to find him a decent home around here.

Several men back at the motel had expressed an interest in adopting the beautiful German Shepherd, but there was something about each individual that made Alex hesitate. In any event, he still had a few days to decide.

In the meantime, Alex went up to the campsite to give Jack a good run. Everybody in Saul's family liked the dog and made a fuss over him, and Jack seemed entranced by little Jimmy who was equally charmed by Jack. Only Nancy was noticeably stand-offish whenever Alex and the dog appeared together.

When Alex and Jack arrived the next day, the camp was abuzz with the news that the following day would be Jimmy's first birthday. Heather and

Dawn had decided that there was no way, with their limited cooking equipment, to bake a cake for him, so somebody would have to go to town and buy one.

Alex volunteered immediately and, after a short conflab, he and Jack were off to Middleton. He might have gone a bit overboard when selecting the size of the cake, but he figured there were a lot of mouths to feed. He went for the chocolate one, picturing Jimmy with his mouth and face smeared with the gooey icing.

He was almost back to the spring when he re-membered candles and had to turn around and go back down. Taking an alternate route back through town, he happened on a spot where a yard sale was in progress. He drove by and then pulled over and walked back, thinking he might find something for the little fellow. The only thing that caught his eye was a Jolly Jumper. The thing looked clean and safe.

"Yes," the woman said, "You could certainly hang it from a tree branch."

When he gave Nancy the gift, they found a suit-able low hanging branch, secured it and put Jimmy in it. They both laughed, leaning into each other, as Jimmy began bouncing and giggling happily.

27: Bandwagon

"Horst, Saul tells me that when you're not busy with your current assignment, you're involved in some pretty interesting research at the university."

Alex poured himself some coffee from the pot on the fire and seated himself at a discrete distance from Horst, who was, as usual, totally nude.

"Yes, yes, Alex, most fascinating. You are a student yourself, so you must be aware of all the historic genetic probes that are going on worldwide?"

"My major was English Lit. and a bit of history. Other than having to memorize that damned DNA sequence in first year Biology 101, I know nothing about the subject."

"Ah, well, let me explain. I came over from Germany to work with Professor Martin. I am now his assistant. The professor is involved in the problem of the Canadian Métis population trying to establish their First Nation status. You are familiar with this situation?"

"No, can't say that I am. Tell me more."

Heather, one of the twin sisters, appeared at the entrance to her tent, smiling and beckoning to Horst.

"I'll be with you shortly," he called to her. "Patience, my pet. Patience."

He turned his attention to Alex. "Professor Martin decided on Nova Scotia as an excellent place for his research. The Acadian Métis are descendants of the first French settlers and Mi'kmaq and intermarriage was common. The professor's project is being funded by the Department of Indian Affairs. They hope that our work will help them with the very difficult problem of determining status."

"How could it be difficult? You either are a Métis or you're not."

"We wish that it was that simple. We focus on DNA and you would think that that would make any inquiries by someone requesting official status to be straightforward. But that's not the case. In 1985 a bill called Bill C-31 was passed. Professor Martin says that it was an attempt by the government to reduce the number of status Indians so that they would only have legal obligations to the declining few. I'm not really interested in the politics of it all. In the meantime, the requests by people who want to establish their aboriginal heritage for one reason or another have got our lab techs working overtime."

"So you're saying that, because my ancestors are from Nova Scotia and their forefathers might have intermarried with the Mi'kmaq, I might have some First Nation blood in me?"

"Oh, mein Gott! Now you're going to jump on that bandwagon."

"I'm just saying—"

"Damn—Heather again. This won't take long."

28: Anything free

Saul Levy looked up from the fire he'd been tending to see two men standing at the edge of the clearing, watching him. One of the men was carrying a rifle.

Saul quickly sized up the situation. Two large, dangerous-looking men, one with a gun and the other fingering the hilt of a large Bowie knife sheathed at his hip, were now walking toward the fire.

The three women present backed away from the fire pit, Nancy moving over to her child, who was laughing and bouncing around in the Jolly Jumper suspended from a tree branch. Horst stood up uncertainly.

Stay calm, Saul said to himself. Aloud he said, "Welcome to our camp, brothers. We're just about to have lunch. Would you like to join us?"

The taller of the intruders spat out a cud of tobacco. "The word around here is that you folks believe in free love. My brother and me plans to sample some of it."

His brother said, "Ya, we likes anything free: free lunch, free beer and, even better, free sex."

Saul leapt to his feet but was driven backwards by

a rifle butt thrust into his gut.

"You settle down now and wait your turn. We's gonna attend to these ladies first. Then my brother, who's a little funny that way, might have a crack at you, too."

He turned to the women. "Now, you girls stop hiding those pretty titties of yours. Take off your tops. Let's have a look atcha."

The women moved defiantly backwards, shielding their breasts. The man with the rifle pointed it skyward and fired it.

"I said, get them goddamned tops off, and do it now."

29: Well-trained

Alex was excited as he left his truck at the edge of the woods and headed along the path toward the little colony, carrying the bag of special things he had purchased for Jimmy. The little guy didn't have any real toys and there wasn't much fun to be had with the sticks, shiny stones and birch bark creations that had been his only amusement. The second-hand Jolly Jumper Alex had found at the yard sale had been a real hit.

Jack jumped out of the truck and ran ahead, dancing around at the entrance to the path, eager to get back to the campsite.

"Heel, you silly bugger. I'll be the leader of this expedition."

The dog flattened his ears and moped a bit but then fell in behind him.

Alex had only gone a few paces into the woods when he heard the shot, and then the sound of the little boy screaming. Jack immediately came to life, bolting forward, hitting Alex on the back of his legs and almost bowling him over.

Alex dropped his bundle. "Stop, Jack! Stop, stop! Come, come, to me!"

Surprisingly, the dog obeyed. "Somebody must have spent a lot of time training you, you rascal. Now sit and stay, and I mean it, stay!"

He began running as fast as he could in the direction of the clearing, only slowing his pace when he began to hear deep, threatening voices mingled with plaintive pleas and the wailing of the child.

Checking back to make sure Jack was still sitting, anxious, but statue-still, Alex made his way carefully to a spot by the edge of the clearing where he knew he wouldn't be seen. He paused for a moment to take in the scene. Two intruders facing away from him were shouting demands to Saul and the women, all of whom were cowering on the other side of the fire.

Before he had really thought anything out, Alex ran forward and hurled himself at the back of the man holding the rifle, knocking him forward into the fire. He landed on top of the man, pressing him down on the red-hot coals.

The big man squirmed and clawed at the surrounding turf, trying to escape. Seconds later, they both rolled, smouldering, a few feet away from the fire pit. Alex, still on top, managed to pull the gun from the man's scorched hands.

The rifle erupted and a stray shot narrowly missed the second man, who immediately drew his hunting knife and made to lunge at Alex.

There was loud snapping and crashing sound as Jack came flying out of the underbrush and leapt into the air, catching the man's wrist in his jaws and clamping down.

The shocked man screamed and dropped his knife, but Jack hung on as he was hurled around in circles until, finally, the man dislodged him. Jack landed with pieces of the man's flesh still caught in his teeth.

The man started running. Recovering his feet, Jack was instantly on him, snarling and biting at his backside and chasing him off into the woods.

Alex shot a brief glance over his shoulder at Jack disappearing as he turned the bigger man's body towards him and pressed the rifle tightly down across his Adam's apple. He held it there for what seemed like an eternity until a gentle hand fell on his shoulder and he heard Saul saying, "Stop, Alex, stop. You're going to kill him!"

At that the red cloud of anger that had been consuming Alex cleared and he lifted the rifle off the man's throat. After a moment he handed it to Saul. He called to Horst, "Bring me that piece of rope, man."

The big man, still stunned, made little effort as Alex flipped him over, pulled his arms roughly into position, and bound his wrists.

"You're under arrest, you asshole."

"Under arrest? Can you do that, Alex?" Saul said.

"Damned right I can, and I am. This is a citizen's arrest and I've got every reason and right to do it. Get out to the truck and get my cellphone. Dial 911. You'll have to explain where we are, and say two people attacked an unarmed group. And pass me back me that rifle!"

30: Sirens

As Saul disappeared running up the path toward the road, Alex pulled the bolt on the ancient Lee Enfield rifle back, ejected the shell and then rammed the one remaining bullet into the chamber.

Where is that idiot with the knife?

"You girls get the baby and stay close to Horst."

Alex spun nervously around scanning the surrounding forest until his attention was drawn to the man on the ground who had come to and was wriggling around, trying to get up. *That's one big bastard —thank god I got his hands tied.*

The man rolled and cursed until finally, lodging himself against the bench that surrounded the fire pit, he was able to use it to prop his torso up and get to his feet.

He turned, staggering wildly around, before moving over and leaning against a tree. Dirt and rivulets of tobacco juice embedded the stubble of his beard, and blood and spittle drooled down over his chin.

Glowering at Alex he began screaming. "Clyde, where the hell are you? Get your ass over here and cut me loose."

Alex moved carefully forward and grabbed the

long, trailing end of the rope that bound the man's hands. He slung it around the tree the man was leaning against.

Horst came to help, and together they wound the rope around the man's torso, securing him firmly in place.

The man continued shouting for his brother, hurling obscenities, and kicking and hurling threats at Alex and Horst.

The women and child cowered together beyond the fire pit, a safe distance away.

Alex and Horst took turns standing guard and trying to comfort the women for what seemed like an eternity before they heard the sound of first one siren and then several others in the distance, getting closer.

The sirens, now close, stopped, and they could hear the sound of several vehicles on the gravel fire road.

Saul came running down the path to the clearing ,with Sgt. Denton of the RCMP close behind and two more constables bringing up the rear. One of them had Jack on an improvised leash. He turned him loose and the dog ran over to Alex's side and sat down, panting, tongue lolling, looking expectantly up at him.

"Good dog, good dog. You're a crazy son of a bitch, but good dog, all the same."

Denton waited while Alex knelt down and patted his dog, checking him over for injuries. Then he went over and stood in front of the man tied to the tree.

"So, we meet again, Homer. Here we are, with you in trouble again. My, oh my, what have you been up to this time? Wait; don't bother telling me until I read you this caution. You are under arrest. You are not obliged to say anything but if you do—Hell, you've heard this so often you could recite it yourself. Anyway, your brother is up in the scout car with Constable Lewis, signing his confession, so it doesn't matter too much what you say right now."

Denton glanced at Alex. "That dog had him treed about half a mile down the road. We'll be taking him down to the hospital to get his wrist and his arse patched up before we put him in the cells."

"It ain't fair, it ain't fair! You know Clyde's a few bricks shy of a load. He'd say anything. We ain't done anything wrong. It's them bloody trespassing hippies. Just look at them and look at me, all burnt and bruised and just because we made a friendly sociable visit."

The sergeant turned to one of the constables. "Jim, take those ropes off Homer and cuff him. Not too tight now. We don't want Mister Leonard to be uncomfortable."

The sergeant watched the constables and their prisoner walk away toward the waiting vehicles before turning to the assembly of men and women. "We're going to need statements from each of you. I don't see any power poles leading into here, and it's going to be dark soon, so you all better come down to the station tomorrow. It's handier when we can use a computer."

Alex watched the policeman walk away, then looked around for Nancy. She and Jimmy were nowhere to be seen.

31: So and So will state

When Alex arrived at the RCMP detachment office the following morning the Volkswagen van was already in the parking lot, empty. Saul, Horst and the women were inside the office waiting for him, but Nancy and Jimmy weren't there. Alex was confused and strangely disappointed by their absence, but said nothing.

Once they were all seated at the conference table, Sgt. Lewis began explaining what would be required of them. "To start with, folks, these are what we call statement forms. If you look at the heading, you will notice that it begins with a sentence that says 'So and So will state'. You are the So and So's and whatever you say on the report, the Crown Attorney will expect you to stand by when you are called as a witness at Homer's trial."

Alex said, "Do we actually have to be present? Aren't these statements enough? I've got to get back to Toronto shortly. Isn't there another way? When will the trial be?"

"That's hard to say. It always takes a while. Homer and Clyde will be arraigned in the next day or so, but, from what I'm hearing, they're both going to plead 'not guilty'. That means the matter will have to go for 'discovery', which is seeing if there's enough facts to make it worth a trial. You're probably looking at several weeks."

"That puts the kibosh on my plans. Are those jerks going to be out on bail and a threat to us?"

"That depends on what the judge decides at the arraignment, but the Crown has indicated to me that, since both of the Leonard boys have lengthy rap sheets, and constitute a danger to the community, he will be looking for a bail amount that will be out of reach for them. So you can rest easy about that. They won't be bothering you anytime soon."

Saul leaned forward over the table. "Not guilty! After what they did, how could they imagine that any court would find them not guilty? Who would have advised them to do that?"

The Mountie chuckled. "Yeah, it is a bit weird. They aren't using a court-appointed attorney. They're using a local guy who fancies himself a kind of paralegal rep. It seems he is going to base his defence on the fact that both of his clients were not trespassing but were on their own land, ejecting interlopers."

Saul said, "What difference would that make? The big bugger was threatening us with a gun. He even fired it."

"I know it sounds ridiculous, but the Crown Attorney feels that he must look into that aspect in case it might make a difference."

Alex looked around the table and then back at the

sergeant. "Would you excuse me for a moment? There's something in my truck I'd like to bring in and show you."

Alex headed out to his truck, opened the door and, shoving Jack aside, reached under the seat for his briefcase. When he returned to where everyone was waiting and plopped the old leather case on the table, they all looked at him curiously.

He pulled out several pieces of paper, placed them in front of the Mountie, and waited for his reaction.

The sergeant read each sheet carefully, "Well I'll be...This is an official registry map of the property, and *this* is a current deed showing that is owned by one Alex Johnson. That's you, isn't it?"

Everyone else stared at Alex with a look of shocked disbelief coloured with the unspoken word 'Why?'

It wasn't something Alex wanted to address in front of the policeman. He said to his friends, "I'll explain it all to you later."

32: Just tell her

"I guess it's like this: you were all so friendly and welcoming that I wanted it to be just because of me, not because you had to suck up to the guy who owned the land. I was really hoping Nancy would be around for this conversation."

It really was none of his business, but Alex couldn't help wondering why Nancy had made herself scarce when the police arrived at the campsite. When he had asked, Saul had just said it was up to Nancy to tell him. "We all know why, but it's her business."

It should have ended there, but Alex couldn't let it go. He had found himself thinking about Nancy a lot since they first met. Her behaviour when the police arrived just added to the mystique surrounding her. He didn't tell Saul about the erotic dream he had had about her.

"Alex, I've noticed the way you look at her when you're up here. I think maybe your wanting to find her is more about how you feel than to find out why she disappeared when the police came. Just tell her. That's always been my policy. If I wanted a woman, even if she was a total stranger, I just went up to her and said, 'I want you horizontal.'"

"Jeezuz! You must have got a lot of slaps on your face."

"Ya, I did, but I got a lot of nookie, too. Just look at those wives of mine over yonder."

"I don't know, Saul."

"Trust me, kid, just do it. Her favourite wine used to be Mateus. You know, the stuff in the chubby green bottles. Why don't you get a bottle and share a drink with her?"

"It's not like that. I just want to know why she was so afraid of the police."

"Sure, sure. Anyway, if by chance you find yourself in the liquor store today, could you pick up two large jugs of red wine and two more of that local Golden Glow cider? We're going to have a celebration to-night."

33: A question

The sun had already begun to set and the shadows from the surrounding trees were closing in when Alex appeared at the campsite, lugging two shopping bags.

There was a look of recognition and a cheer from the group gathered around the crackling fire.

Alex placed the bags close to where Saul was sitting and found a seat on the log beside him while Jack went over to Dawn and flipped over on his back, wagging his tail in anticipation of a good belly rub.

Each time Saul reached into one of the bags and extracted a bottle of wine or cider there was a quiet cheer and clapping. When, at last, he brought out not one, but two bottles of Mateus, there was a hush and an exchange of knowing looks.

Alex cast a sheepish glance across the fire, expecting to see Nancy among the women, but she wasn't there.

Soon the enamel mugs were out, and everyone was helping themselves. Alex decided to sample the Golden Glow, figuring the cider would be less intoxicating. He wanted to have his wits about him if he got the chance to talk to Nancy.

Where the hell is she?

It was while he was sipping his third mug of cider that it occurred to him that the word 'hard' when applied to cider was probably a word of caution. He was feeling no pain, and found himself laughing at Jack as he tried to wrestle a stick out of Heather's hands.

When Saul suggested that he should sample some of the wine as well, Alex replied, "I don't mish my drings."

Saul figured it might be time for Plan B. He passed a bottle of Mateus to Alex.

"Take this up to Nancy's tent. She's been sitting up there in a snit all evening. I told her you were curious about why she took off when the police came up here."

"Whadid she shay?"

"She told me to tell you to mind your own business. But I don't think she really meant it. Here, take your peace offering and head up there. Jimmy is asleep in Dawn's tent."

Staggering up the knoll, Alex went over what he was going to say. "So sorry, didn mean to upshet you. Thish is for you. How abouda dring?"

When he got to where Nancy was sitting in front of her pup tent, Alex tried to say something.

She beat him to the punch. "Okay, so you've been kind and generous to all of us but that doesn't give you the right to pry into my life. I don't ask you about yours, so just leave it."

Spying the bottle, she cracked a smile and said,

"Give me that damned thing!"

She grabbed the bottle and took a long swig. "Ah, I needed that. Now take the rest of it and piss off."

"Ash you wiz, my dear. But before I go, would you show me one small cursy?"

"What?" She got to her feet.

"Is about them damned long dreshes you're always wearing. I keep wondering about your legs. If it's not too much trouble, could I see them?"

This was not the question Nancy had anticipated, and it certainly wasn't the one Alex had planned to ask. The two of them let it hang in the air for a moment before they broke into laughter.

Catching her breath, Nancy said, "If it's that important to you—feast your eyes, boyo."

She hiked her skirt up and Alex just stared. They were the most beautiful things he had ever seen. It was common knowledge around campus back in Toronto that he had a leg fetish, and over the years of personal hands-on research, he had become a bit of an expert on the subject.

Transfixed, Alex stumbled forward into Nancy's arms. Bracing himself on her shoulders, he found himself face to face with her and, without thinking, he kissed her full on the mouth.

"Whoa! What was that?" she said, pushing him away.

He stepped back and was about to apologize when Jack's barking and a voice calling from down at the campsite interrupted him.

It was Dawn. Jimmy was awake and needed his

mother.

Alex spent an uncomfortable hour and a half talking with Saul and Marina and drinking black coffee until he felt sober enough to drive back to the motel.

Once in the truck, he shouted, "Shit, shit, shit! How stupid was that, now? I've spoiled everything. They'll think I'm an idiot and Nancy will never speak to me again. Legs? Where the hell did that come from? I was supposed to ask her about hiding from the police."

Turning to comfort Jack, who was upset and confused, he said, "But all the same, they're a helluva set of gams!"

34: Someone knocking

Alex made his way cautiously back to Middleton and parked the old truck. With Jack in tow, he aimed for his room and, once there, flopped down onto his bed.

He'd been lying on the bed passed out for about an hour when he was awakened by Jack scratching at him and licking his face.

"Not now, for chrissake, Jack, my head is splitting —leave me alone."

But the dog persisted, and Alex opened one eye to take in Jack madly wagging his tail and barking at the door. Someone was knocking.

"Okay, okay, Jack, I'm coming. Probably that damned night clerk. Maybe I left the lights on in the truck again."

He opened the door and Jack rushed out, nearly bowling over Nancy, who stood there with the other bottle of wine in her hand.

35: Pillow talk

It was raining the following day, and Alex and Nancy were lying in her tent, side by side.

"Where do I begin, Alex? Well, first of all I want you to know that you were sleeping with a married woman last night. That's if my divorce hasn't gone through, and I can't imagine that it has. If you're not okay with that, just let me know and we'll call this off and you won't need to know any more."

"Are you nuts? Get over here!"

Alex tried to pull her over to him but she gently pushed him back to his side of the tent. "Not now; I need to tell you this."

Alex forced himself to lie back and listen. "Hit me, Nancy. How bad can this be?"

"It's not funny. My life is in danger and if we don't stop this now, yours will be, too. My husband wants to find Jimmy and me and kill us. He told me, so I took off the moment I could. Saul and his family have been hiding us and keeping us safe."

"Why would he want to kill you?"

"He's crazy. He wasn't always crazy. He was a normal, sane man before they shipped him off to Kuwait."

"He was a soldier?"

"We were both in the forces. We got married just before he shipped out, and when I knew that Jimmy was on the way I resigned and settled in to wait for him to return. It was meant to be a storybook marriage. I spent my time decorating and furnishing our PMQ and basking in all the attention and care I was getting from the other military wives."

"What's a PMQ?"

"Private married quarters. You must have seen all those lookalike little houses clustered around the Base down in Greenwood."

She paused a moment. "This whole thing gets kind of complicated. Do you really want to know all the details?"

"I want to know everything about you."

"Well, if you won't let it go, it's like this: my last name now is Jackson. It used to be Thomas, and I wish it was again. Mark and I were both in the forces. The thing is, Mark belonged to a very special branch of the service called Canadian Special Operations, or Special Op. He was a sniper, and not just any sniper; he was the best shot in the Canadian military. Because he was so good with a rifle, they promoted him beyond the expectations of his other qualifications and put him in charge of recruiting suitable candidates to serve with Special Op. It didn't matter which branch of the service a likely soldier, airman or even sailor was in, so that's why we ended up at Greenwood."

She sat up to continue the story. Alex found it hard

to concentrate on her words at first, but he bore down. *The story won't go on forever.*

"Most of the men, and even a couple of the women he worked with, were hunters and woodsmen with great eyesight and steady nerves. He found some new guys in the area and was heavily involved in their training on the range and in the woods up on South Mountain. Then he got the news that he was to be deployed to a potential trouble spot to head up a special squad on a Joint Task Force. He wouldn't tell me where. That was just a month or so before Iraq invaded Kuwait, and I found out later that he had been lying in wait in the desert with a squad of his American and British cohorts, preparing to take out the leading officers of Saddam Hussein's Special Republican Guard that was spearheading the invasion."

She looked away as if seeing something, then looked back at Alex.

"Something happened there and there was so much secrecy about it that I guess I'll never know what. All I know is that I said goodbye to a wonderful, sane husband and got back a broken-spirited violent madman. I think he was in over his head. He thought he was going to join the ranks of the famous snipers he so admired and never tired of talking about. He even treasured the photographs of people like Francis Pegahmagabow, who killed 378 Germans in World War I, and Harold Marshal from WWII.

"But there was a big difference between those men and Mark. He performed some of the longest perfect shots ever executed on the range in simulated combat circumstances, but they were just targets. He'd never shot a living thing—he didn't even hunt."

"So why would they send him?"

"God knows, Alex, I don't. All I know is that whatever occurred, it was serious enough that he was facing a court martial and threatening to kill me and Jimmy."

"Why did he blame you and Jimmy for whatever happened to him over there?"

"This is where you start looking funny at me, but I guess if you find it hard to believe what I'm about to tell you, you won't be the first. Mark and I were engaged for over a year. I know it was a stupid, old fashioned idea but I made up my mind that I would not have serious sex with him until we were married. He was a devout Catholic and seemed content with the arrangement. For my part, I was fed up with all the sexual harassment so many of us women in the services were subjected to, so I decided to take a stand. I didn't want to be part of any sordid situation. We fooled around a lot, but that was all. We decided on a wedding date and got the Commander's permission and a license a couple of months in advance.

"Mark had become friends with the Catholic chaplain, and he was keen to conduct the wedding whenever, and that was just as well because Mark only got a couple of days' notice before his deployment. We settled on having the ceremony the day before he was due to leave. It seemed like a romantic idea, creating a wonderful memory to sustain us both during his absence.

"It was a simple ceremony, with just the chaplain and three of the men Mark had been teaching. We all went over to Mess afterwards to celebrate. We were both excited and nervous as hell, so we left the party as soon as possible and headed to the motel room in Kingston."

She grinned and looked away. "Mark was so excited he sort of exploded prematurely, before he even...! After that he was so embarrassed that he couldn't do anything else, then or the next morning. We clung together through the night, with him constantly apologizing and me assuring him that everything would be all right. We would make up for the lost time when he got back."

Her smile was long gone. "That didn't happen because something else happened. A month after he left, I wasn't feeling well, particularly in the mornings, so I went to see the doctor. I nearly fainted when he told me that I was pregnant. It wasn't possible, nothing had really happened. When I told the doctor the circumstances, he gave me a more thorough examination and verified what I had said. He had heard of this sort of thing happening but this was the first time he had ever encountered it. I was still a virgin, everything was intact, but there was no getting away from the fact that I was definitely pregnant."

Alex had at least thirty-seven questions. He managed to hold them in.

"When I told Mark, he went ballistic—he would not believe me at all. He was convinced that I had had an affair. Whatever had driven him crazy back on the sands of Kuwait, his absurd notion of my infidelity amplified it and he was in a murderous mood.

"He had asked one of his buddies to watch over me while he was away. Keith and his wife, Mary, were always there for me when I needed help. It was a long haul before his tour would be over but there was lots of support for me. When I got word he was on his way home earlier than expected, I was excited and thankful. Nobody explained why he was coming home early, and I didn't think to ask. I couldn't wait for him to see Jimmy.

"We were waiting by the runway when his plane landed, but he slipped away with a bunch of his buddies and headed over to the Mess. It was close to midnight before he came home and flopped down on the couch, never saying a word. In the morning, I had Jimmy in his highchair, coffee made and breakfast all ready for him, eager to begin our new life together, but he just stuck his head in the kitchen and said, 'I'm outta here. I'll find somewhere else to bunk in.'

"He didn't even look at his son."

Alex opened his mouth, thought better of saying anything, and closed it again.

"I was stunned; I couldn't believe what was happening. I didn't know what to do. I called Mary but she could barely talk. She was beside herself: Keith was in the hospital because Mark had attacked him, accusing him of having an affair with me and fathering Jimmy.

"He never told the MPs who had beaten him up. It was only when they tracked down some of the other fellows who were there at the time and found out what had happened that they started looking for Mark. They caught him trying to leave the Base that morning, after he left the house, and now were holding him in the cells. I couldn't believe it. Who was this man? Not my Mark. I didn't understand any of it. I just hoped that Mary and Keith would be all right because you never know with the military. They might well have released Mark again. Many of the MPs and most of the senior officers were his friends and they would believe his side of the story. They would have considered his assault on Keith a crime of passion and worthy of special consideration. Why hadn't he said anything to me?

"Father Crosby came to the house to talk to me. He had heard Mark's confession after the fight with Keith, I guess. Father Crosby said he would never be able to tell me or anyone else what Mark had said to him, but he was concerned for my safety. He wanted to know if there was anywhere I could go for a while.

"My family is all in Saskatchewan. The only one I could think of who might put us up for a while was my friend, Mirna, in Halifax. Father Crosby helped me pack up a few things and saw me off, giving me all the information I would need to keep in touch. I needed to know what exactly was happening, that was for sure."

She shifted as if to get up, then settled again. "I was so nervous I forgot to look at the gas gauge on my car and the damned thing sputtered to a stop on the highway halfway between Kingston and Berwick. I was sobbing uncontrollably and poor little Jimmy was wailing in his car seat when Saul's van pulled up beside me. I guess you can figure out the rest of the story."

~

Father Patrick Crosby, a tall red-headed man in his early thirties, felt that being a Catholic chaplain in the Canadian Armed Forces was a good gig. When he was not wearing his collar or dressed in his ceremonial attire at the front of his church, he happily appeared to be just another young officer. He was especially pleased with his assignment to the small chapel at 14 Wing Greenwood Air Force Base in the Annapolis Valley.

His flock was small and constantly changing as members of his congregation were reassigned and moved to different locations, but he loved living in the area. When not attending to his parish duties he was free to pursue his love of sports. He was an excellent athlete and his prowess on the Base hockey team earned him the nickname "The Flying Father". He loved hiking on the two mountains above the base, carrying either his camera or his shotgun.

Because of the transient nature of the members of his congregation, making permanent friends was a bit of a problem, so when he encountered people for whom he had a particular affection, he tried to make the best of the limited time he knew he would have in their company.

Mark Jackson, a member of the Special Forces assigned to the Base, and Nancy, his fiancée, were a couple he took to right away. Mark was a devout Catholic and he was helping Nancy to convert. They both attended Mass regularly and were part of any of the church social events. Father Crosby became a regular guest at the dinners the couple hosted at the mess and the three of them had become close friends.

He was particularly intrigued with Mark's special status and assignments. Mark invited him to join him for target practice on the shooting range and the priest was astounded by the incredible feats of accuracy he performed and the high esteem in which his riflery students held him.

Father Crosby knew that firing a shot or two himself might look a little out place for a priest, but he decided to throw caution to the wind and accepted a .22 calibre target rifle from Mark. "Praise the Lord and pass the ammunition!" he said.

Other than when Mark was attending Mass or at confession, he felt that they were simply the best of friends.

When Mark told him that he was going to ship out for a special assignment, he couldn't say where, and that he and Nancy wanted to be married right away, he pulled out all the stops, foregoing all traditional formalities, and arranged a quick, quiet service. He promised Mark that he would look out for Nancy's well-being while he was away.

He also promised to keep in touch with him, since he knew he would have better official channels to use while Mark was on a sensitive mission than Nancy would. He was a willing go-between.

Even with his connections, communications between Mark and him were infrequent and the return letters riddled with security redactions. Nancy received no letters from Mark and was totally dependent on Father Crosby for news.

Then Nancy shared the news that she was three months pregnant, hoping he could somehow get the joyous news to Mark.

Father Crosby was never able to confirm that his letter to Mark in that regard had ever found him, but after his return, Mark's strange actions seemed to confirm that it had.

When Mark returned to Greenwood, he went straight to the church and rang the bell for the confessional. It was only later that Father Crosby learned from Nancy that he hadn't even gone home first. Mark was different than the man who had left —a shell of his former self. He spent an hour in the confessional, first skipping over what he had done to Keith, then spewing out, in details so horrible that Father Crosby was thankful that rules of the confessional would never allow him to reveal them, stories which implicated Mark in incidents of murder. These were serious war crimes, but one disclosure of in-tent he made regarding Nancy and her child set Father Crosby weighing his vows against the common-sense action that would prevent harm to an innocent woman and her child.

When he sensed Mark was finished, he suggested that he wait a moment so they could pray together. What else could he say? A few Hail Marys and some simple act of penance wouldn't cover this. He crossed himself, made a brief appeal to God, then parted the curtain and went to join him.

Mark, however, was nowhere in sight.

Panicking about what Mark might do, Father Crosby headed directly to the house where Nancy and Jimmy were waiting expectantly. He told her just enough, and said that she would just have to trust his judgment. He handed her a list of phone numbers where she could reach him at any time.

He then headed to the Military Police post at the entrance to the Base, determined to convey what he knew, oath or no oath.. But that did not prove necessary—his Lord had intervened.

Maybe I shouldn't have panicked and sent Nancy fleeing?

But later, the sergeant in charge told him that, after a brief hearing with a pre-court-martial panel of officers, Mark might well be released on his own recognizance. Father Crosby knew that God had sent him in the right direction when he went to warn her.

The sergeant wasn't forthcoming other than to tell him that, as they spoke, Mark was being taken away to an undisclosed location for further interrogation.

Father Crosby had no way of contacting Nancy with what might have been slightly better news—she was already on her way. He would have to wait for her to contact him.

36: Discovery

Only the concerned participants in the case of The Crown vs Homer Leonard were gathered in the courtroom in Kentville. Alex was busy explaining to Saul and the girls that what they were about to participate in was only a discovery hearing.

"It's only if the judge decides that the evidence merits it, that the case will go forward. The formal trial will be held later, but don't worry because—"

There was a sudden loud banging of judge's gavel and the courtroom fell silent.

"I appear for the accused, Your Honour," a short, obese man said. He wore a vintage blue suit with a gaping jacket, a yellowed white shirt that was threatening to pop its buttons and a stubby tie. His trousers were hauled up close to his armpits and held in place by a pair of sturdy red suspenders.

Judge Pierce glowered down over his spectacles and inquired, "And who might you be?"

"My name is Nigel Lardsome, Your Honour."

At that, the court clerk seated in front of the lofty bench piped up, "How do you spell that?"

"Just the way it sounds, sir: N-I-G-E-L."

"No, I mean the last name."

"Same thing: just the way it sounds"

"Okay…" the clerk drawled.

The judge said, "Are you a lawyer, sir?"

"Naw, Your Honour. I'm just a friend looking after him—he's kinda shy."

"Mr., ah, Lardsome, your client is facing some very serious charges. I see here that Mr. Leonard has declined the service of a court-appointed attorney in favour of you, but I don't see a document signifying that you have preregistered as an agent, so I guess we should postpone these proceedings until you do."

At that the Crown Attorney stood. "I have no objection to Mr. Lardsome representing Mr. Leonard. I have seen him defending people with traffic offences in Magistrate's court. He's a bit of an unofficial paralegal when he's not working at his full-time milk delivery job."

The judge scratched his head and reluctantly acceded. "I guess as long as it's all right with you, there's no need to take up more of the court's time."

Alex could imagine the judge thinking, *Here we go again, another tiresome busybody.*

The hearing proceeded as expected, with Nigel Lardsome giving his interpretation of Perry Mason, pausing, gesticulating, pontificating and asking inane questions of the accused and other witnesses and acting woebegone and set-upon when he didn't like the answers.

All the defence's false claims were easily discredited under cross examination, and in a record three hours the yawning judge called the proceedings to a halt. Alex, Saul and the other four women sat, anxiously awaiting the judge's decision.

Judge Pierce began to speak, but stopped when the child one of the women was holding began to cry. He waited until the child settled down, then said, "Having heard the evidence and the testimony of both the defence and the prosecution, it's clear to me that this matter should proceed to trial. The clerk informs me that the trial date will be two months hence, on July 18. The accused will be remanded into custody until that time."

Homer Leonard leapt to his feet. "What about bail? What about my fucking bail? Lardsome, you promised you'd bail me outta here, you fat bastard!"

Gathering his files and placing them in his briefcase, the wannabe lawyer looked up at the judge and spoke for the last time, "I promised him nothing of the sort, Your Honour."

Having had enough of the whole affair, the judge slammed down his gavel and two sheriff's officers dragged Homer Leonard, kicking and screaming obscenities, away and down to the cells.

~

"I want to run something by you, Saul," Alex said on their way back up the mountain. "I might be crazy, but I'm thinking of bidding on the old blacksmith's place at the auction next week. Every time I pass the place on the way up here, I feel guilty. I know my grandfather would be appalled at the state it's in and his father, Ben, has probably already rolled over in his grave. I thought maybe I could buy it, tear it down and clean up the junk around it and plant some grass and trees on it. You know, make it respectable."

"What would you do with it then, Alex? Are you planning to flip it and make a profit?"

"No! Why would you think that?"

"No offence. I guess it's just in my blood. I've told you that my family is in the land speculation business back in New York. Anyway, you'd have trouble getting a mortgage; the banks don't like taking land as collateral."

"I don't need to get a mortgage. I'd be financing it myself."

"You could handle that? Who knew?"

"Never mind that. What do you think? Should I try to buy the place?"

"Tell you what: why don't we go down to the graveyard and see what they think?"

They left the truck in its normal spot and made their way down the winding path. When they arrived at the cemetery, Alex paused while Saul went directly over to Ben Johnson's headstone.

Alex had seen the mumbo jumbo that went on at the Sunrise Ceremony and was anticipating some sort of similar incantation, but Saul just rested his hand on the cold granite, bowed his head for a few seconds, then looked up and said, "Good. He's in."

37: Auction day

Saul claimed he knew all about the auction business. His father's firm had acquired hundreds of properties through tax sales.

"The first thing we have to do, Alex, is check with the Sheriff's office and find out what the local rules and regulations are. I'm sure they aren't all that different from the rules back in the States. These things all originate from British common law."

After he and Alex left the office in Kentville with a sheaf of official papers, Saul insisted that he go over them carefully. After a thorough study, he said, "Like I told you, the rules are pretty much the same as the ones my father's firm encounters. The one thing that sticks out and seems a little different is that in Nova Scotia you can drive by the property, but you can't go onto the property or into any buildings before the auction. Go figure! Anyway, the rest of the stuff is the same as I am used to."

Saul thought for a moment, getting the steps in order, then said, "We will have to go to the registry office and make sure there are no liens on the property and what the zoning is. That old garage and junkyard might have some environmental concerns, so you better keep that in mind. In one way, you are kind of lucky because it says the municipality is not responsible for the eviction of anybody still living on the property. You would have to do it yourself. I don't think you would want to take that fucker Homer Leonard on again."

"You got that right. And you're coming with me to the auction!"

"It will be my pleasure. But first we better figure out what the place is worth. You are going to pay up front as soon as the auctioneer says, 'Sold.' I don't see it bringing very much unless the Oak Island treasure is buried under all that scrap metal."

"I thought I'd bring twenty thousand cash as a deposit. It says I have three days to come up with the difference."

"Jesus, man, this is Nova Scotia, not Toronto. There's a fifteen-hundred-dollar tax bill and I'll be surprised if it brings more than three thousand."

"Maybe so, but I'll bring that much. If I don't need it, the bank won't object to getting the difference back."

~

A dozen or so cars and trucks lined the side of the road in front of the dilapidated garage that had once been Alex's great-grandfather's blacksmith shop. Alex and Saul were the last to arrive and the auction was just about to start. Everybody else had been there for some time and had had plenty of time to view the property and its dubious contents, but Saul had advised Alex to hold off and not appear too anxious.

Six men were gathered around the auctioneer who had positioned himself inside the large garage door. He was a tall man, a bit stooped, in his late seventies, with slicked-back grey hair. He tapped his microphone to make sure it was working.

It was starting to spit a light rain, so the auctioneer backed further into the building to make more room and said, "Everybody inside, everybody inside." Then spotting two men, he knew from the French Shore, said even louder, "Tout le monde à l'interieur." He looked around smugly, proud of the one sentence that he had memorized in French.

Saul spotted Nigel Lardsome instantly and whispered in Alex's ear, "That's the bugger you're going to have to watch. Did you notice the way he was sucking around the auctioneer when we came in. They know each other and he is looking for some special treatment. The same thing goes on in New York. I've seen it hundreds of times when I went to auctions with my dad."

"What do you mean?"

"That guy is either hoping that the auctioneer will slam his gavel down early so he gets a bargain, or that he's shilling for the registered owner."

"What does shilling mean?"

"Christ, you are naive. I thought you grew up in the city. A shill is someone who boosts the price for the owner. He continues bidding for as long as someone is stupid enough to keep going higher. But he has to be careful because he doesn't really want to buy it, he just wants to fleece extra money out of someone. That porky bugger is either trying to buy the property himself or roasting a mark.'

"Right…?"

"Not now, Alex, it's starting."

The man with the microphone was a real chanting auctioneer, not like the frequently-appointed sheriffs who monotonously said the necessary words. Alex felt himself falling for his rhythmic spell and started to raise his hand, but Saul grabbed his wrist and held it firm.

"Just wait—let them get the low bidders done and out of the way."

Saul was right. In a matter of minutes, the fury of the early bidding subsided, with a dozen disappointed bidders dropping out and kicking stones.

Then the portly man looked knowingly toward the auctioneer and offered his first, and what he obviously hoped would be his last, bid. "Fifteen hundred."

"Now! Alex, now," Saul whispered.

Alex raised it to sixteen. Lardsome immediately went to seventeen hundred.

The rest of the crowd looked on in wonder as a rapid back and forth sent the number soaring up to two thousand dollars. It was Alex's turn to raise the bid but Saul grabbed his hand and spun him around, making it look like he was done and about to leave.

The auctioneer lapsed into his final call. "All

through, all done, any advance on a bid of two thousand?"

Alex squirmed to get out of Saul's grip but his friend held him tight until he heard the auctioneer say "Going once!" Then he let go.

Alex spun around. "Twenty-one hundred dollars."

Lardsome's face went slack. Then he pressed his lips together and shook his head at the auctioneer.

After performing all the necessary rituals, the auctioneer said, "Sold!" and congratulated Alex.

Nigel Lardsome pushed his way up to Alex, who declined the man's proffered hand. Lardsome affected a hurt look and then spoke. "I heard the auctioneer call you Mr. Johnson. Well, Mr. Johnson, good luck with your purchase. I sure hope those old wrecks on the property haven't leaked too much oil into the ground—them cleanups can get expensive."

Then he sneered, turned and waddled away.

Saul mumbled in his wake, "I didn't think you could get that fat on a diet of sour grapes."

38: City slicker eyes

It was a stroke of luck. Alex thought he was going to have to search the Yellow Pages for somebody with the expertise and equipment needed to handle the demolition of the old blacksmith shop and the cleanup of the junk that was all around the place, but, as it turned out, all he had to do was mention what he was looking for to Martha at the motel diner. She wasn't long dragging a burly fellow from a table at the far end of the room and introducing him.

"This is Stanley Bergen. If you're looking for someone with heavy equipment—if you know what I mean—Stanley's your man."

Then Martha winked and wiggled her way back toward the kitchen.

Stanley followed Alex's truck back up to the property, hopped out and strolled around for a while before he offered an appraisal.

"It's a hell of a mess, but you might be in luck when it comes to all those wrecked vehicles. The crusher pulled into Gibson's Auto Salvage yard two days ago and I'm sure they could handle most of that stuff. You might even get a few bucks for them. We can doze the scrap metal up into piles and there are at least two fellows in the area that'll buy it. Don't just take the first offer; let them all bid on it before you sell. Now, let's have a look at that building."

The two men walked slowly over to the shop, and Alex waited while Stanley put his shoulder to a back door and forced his way in. Alex followed a few steps behind.

It was the first time he had entered the building. He had hoped he would never have to. All he wanted was to have the sagging insult to his family's heritage removed. He planned to have the whole site cleared, tilled up and planted with grass and trees.

Stanley pushed his way through the accumulated junk in the interior until he reached the large folding garage door at the front of the building. "Give me a lift with this, Alex. It's a heavy sonofabitch."

The two men struggled with the door unsuccessfully for some time until Stanley finally went over and retrieved an old two by four. Together they were able to lever the door up to its full height.

The room filled with morning light and exposed the two partially-dismantled tractors which they had to push past. Alex rushed back out the large door for a breath of fresh air, but Stanley remained inside for several minutes.

When he reappeared out front he said something that Alex had not been prepared to hear. "You know, I can bring my excavator up here and have this building down in a matter of minutes, but it seems like a shame. They don't build buildings like this anymore. It's post and beam and there's still a lot of good old eight by eights in place. If a fella took the notion he could, with some hard work, restore this old beauty."

"Well, Stanley, it's like they say. Beauty is in the eye of the beholder and I'm not seeing it. That's not the plan, so when can you start the work? I've got to get back to Ontario and I want the place looking respectable before I go."

"I need to check a thing or two, but I should be able to start by the end of the week."

With that, Alex said goodbye to Stanley and headed his truck back to Middleton and the diner for a bite to eat. As he drove along, however, Stanley's words ran around in his head.

By the time he had gone back to his room, cleaned up and headed in for a meal, there was Stanley, sitting with the other fellows, just waiting for a further few words.

"You know, Alex, you can hire me to level the whole thing and make your pretty park. Or, on the other hand, you could spend a hell of a lot of money for my time and the materials for me to make that old beauty shipshape. Or you could do it yourself. Looking at it another way, the stuff that needs to be done to bring it all back isn't rocket science. Even a goof from Upper Canada like you should be able to handle it."

"Well, thanks for the vote of confidence, you old crank."

Alex had become comfortable with the warm-hearted mutual abuse that everybody practised at the diner. He saw his inclusion in the practice as a sign of acceptance.

"Anyway," Stanley said, "why the hell would you spend a shit load on money and material when you got more than you need right there on the property? After a bite let's head back up there, and I'll show you what you haven't been seeing with those city slicker eyes."

When they got back to the property, Stanley grabbed Alex's arm, guided him around to the back of the old building and pointed up the mountain. "Take a look up yonder, my boy. There's enough gol-darned prime old growth red spruce to build a sub-division, if you wanted."

"Oh, I don't know, Stanley, I—"

"All you're going to need is a chain saw, an axe, a peavey and a good yard horse."

"Horse?"

"Yes, a horse, dummy. How the hell do you think you're going to get the logs down here so they can be sawed? And I know a woman who has just the horse you need. It was a gift to her, and it isn't suitable for the riding lessons she gives. She's looking to pass it on to a good home. She claims it's broke to ride and drive and has worked in the woods for several sea-sons. I'll write down her address."

"Whoa! Slow down. I'm not sure I want to take this on, and I'm not sure I know how to handle a yard horse."

"You just said 'whoa' and that was a good start. My services are very expensive, but the advice is free, and you can call on me any time you want to. I'll enjoy coming over here to see how badly you're mucking things up. Now I gotta go, so think it over and let me know."

Alex let Jack into the truck and headed up the mountain to the campsite. He wanted Saul's opinion, but as he was driving along, he realized that he had almost made up his mind to take on the challenge.

Saul was instantly on board, eager to help. But the thing that convinced Alex that the building project would be time well spent was the sight of Nancy and Jimmy hovering nearby.

39: All about Saul

Alex and Saul Levy had very little in common, not much to build a foundation for a new friendship. Nevertheless, it was beginning to happen.

"I had an uncle called Saul," Alex confessed.

Saul replied, "Everybody should have at least one Jewish uncle called Saul. I presume he is Jewish."

"Was Jewish. I put stones on his grave before I left Toronto."

"My God, Alex. Do you think just because you die, you aren't Jewish anymore?"

"Never thought about it like that before, but I guess you're right."

"Of course I'm right. Just because your ancestors down there in the graveyard are dead doesn't mean they give up their religion. If you don't believe me, come down there with me and I'll ask them."

"That won't be necessary, Saul. I know you chat with them, so I'll just stay here and take your word for it. Anyway, as grateful as I am for all the care you have been giving to my ancestors' final resting place, I can't help wondering how you found this land and decided to stay."

"First, my friend, I better explain why I am here

and not back home in the Big Apple on the other side of the border. A text book would call the way we live a hippie subculture. I'm not even sure what 'hippie' means, but I guess everybody needs a label. Anyway our fundamental ethos—"

"What the hell does 'ethos' mean?"

"Pardon me, Alex. I was under the assumption that you had an education! It just means a philosophy, a way of looking at things. Let that sink in, then I'll continue. By definition we are supposed to live in harmony with nature and be into communal living, artistic experimentation, especially music, sexual experimentation and the use of recreational drugs. All of which I plead guilty to. The current movement began in the 60s, but I never made the leap until '79. There was about a million of us young Americans—mostly white, college-educated with homes in the suburbs."

"Okay, I get it. But what brought you to this spot? The camp looks temporary; you couldn't have been living permanently here. You would have been noticed."

"That's true Alex. How do I explain this? Do you know what a pow wow is?"

"Yes, I do." *Christ, where the hell is he going with this now?*

"Well, part of getting back to nature necessitates adopting many of the customs of the First Nations people. For years many of the isolated communes in the Valley have met here to exchange ideas, sing, dance and generally socialize, and maybe meet new people. Sort of a pow wow."

"But why here?"

"We always had the gathering here because it's close to the Spring and that water has become very special to us. Sadly, over the years most of the families have disbanded and gone back to 'civilization', and we are mostly on our own when we come here."

"So when you're not here, where is your permanent home?"

"Up until a few weeks ago we had our own little village in a clearing in the woods down towards the South Shore. People used to joke that we were so far back in the woods that we would have to come out to go hunting. We didn't hunt, but I guess it amused people to say it. The truth is we would go months without ever seeing a stranger, and then it would only be a hunter or fisherman who had lost his bearings and wandered too far away from his camp.

"Supplies were never a problem for us and money was never an issue. I guess I was what the Victorian era people termed a Remittance Man. My wealthy family in New York was always sending me money, much of which, considering my frugal lifestyle, I really didn't need. Most of our supplies were brought into our lake by float plane in the summer or ski plane in the winter. When it was absolutely necessary, one of us would hoof it to the nearest store. Our chickens, goats and garden kept us supplied with all the fresh food we needed."

Saul was silent for a moment, his mind elsewhere. Then he gave himself a little shake. "Our one family outing was our annual trip to this campsite. That's where Marina and I met Heather and Dawn, four years ago. It was good, it was great. Everything was going our way, except no babies…"

"What do you mean *was* going our way?"

"We came down here earlier this year to pay respects and get a few jugs of the Spa water to take back with us. When we got back home there was no home. The three geodesic domes that we had built were burnt to the ground and the chickens and goats set loose and nowhere to be found. There was nothing left, and we were pretty scared by it all, so we came back here to figure out what to do next."

"So what caused the fire? Was it lightning?"

"No, no way. Maybe redneck lightning. I have no proof, but I think it had something to do with the fact that all the Crown land around us had been opened for harvesting. As the logging got closer to us we started protesting and closing off the access roads. In any event, there's nothing there for us, so we'll just have to start all over again somewhere else. This felt like the safest spot for the meantime."

"Hell, you're welcome to stay at the campground —you could build some permanent structures there before winter sets in again."

"Thanks, Alex, but that wouldn't work for us. We need some really remote location. We might even consider somewhere in South America."

"Shit, I don't think that's such a good idea. We don't need another Jonestown."

"Very funny, but don't worry about us. We don't

even like Koolaid. We'll find something suitable...but if it's all right with you, we'll hang out up on the mountain for a while."

"Not a problem, my friend. I'll even make a deal with you. If you agree to take this pesky dog off my hands, I'll sign the place over to you."

"Tempting, but I see something about your relationship with that dog that you have yet to appreciate and own. That dog is *your* dog and will always be just your dog. So get used to it."

At that Jack who had been lying curled up at their feet, reared up excitedly and placed his paws on Alex, licking his face.

Saul laughed and said, "I rest my case."

40: Horseflesh

Alex hadn't bothered to tell Stanley that he had worked with his grandfather in the woods and was no stranger to a hammer and saw; better to let him think he was a quick study. He'd really be surprised when he saw how handy Alex was with horses and he decided that the gift horse would be the first on his list of things to arrange.

The following day Alex and Jack made the trip further down the Valley to a little, secluded homestead on the mountain. Olga, the woman who owned the place, greeted him warmly and showed him around her place. He, to the woman's pleasure, recognized and identified several Icelandic horses in her paddock. A tall, dark-bay mare stood several hands above the little herd, and he realized why the big animal would have been out of place in a riding class.

They started talking horse, sharing experiences, and Alex could tell that she was getting comfortable with the idea of passing the big mare on to him. But it was when he let Jack out of the truck and the woman saw how the man and his dog interacted that she made up her mind. Queenie would be his.

He could have hired a horse trailer to pick up his

new charge, but the idea of riding the horse along the ridge of the North Mountain slowly to see a little more of the country appealed to him. He would drive back and leave the truck and Jack with his friends, then catch the bus along Route 1 to where he could walk to Olga's. Then he could start the long ride back.

It would take the better part of a day to get back to the campsite above the smithy, where a newly constructed temporary shelter and corral were waiting for Queenie.

41: Ancestral home

"Good afternoon, Mr. Lardsome. Is there something I can do for you?"

The now-familiar man had pushed his way into the motel diner and, a folder in hand, wedged himself into the booth seat opposite Alex.

"Mr. Johnson, I'm glad our paths have crossed again, because I've got some information that I'm sure you will be interested in. I hope there are no hard feelings about our last encounter. The magistrate said I was a busybody. Hell, I've been called worse. The truth is I'm just a curious person who feels that he should be there for his neighbours. That's why I came to find you."

Lardsome picked up the folder, straightened the stack of papers inside it, and set it down on the table. Alex was reminded of the thing the magician does with this hand when he doesn't want you to watch the other hand.

Lardsome patted the folder and said, "I just love going through old records. Deeds, death certificates, census records—it's incredible what you can learn. For example, when I was doing the extended title search on the property you outbid me on the other day, I happened on something that might interest you. You probably know that that property once belonged to your great grandfather, Ben Johnson, and his wife, Lilly, who was a Leonard. This is where it gets interesting. You may not know that, among my other credentials, I am a licensed real estate agent. Now get this: I have as part of my listings a large property up on North Mountain belonging to one Wilbur Leonard. It turns out Wilbur shares a great grandfather with you, so he'd be your second cousin. It immediately occurred to me that, since you seem to be buying up property in the area, you might be interested in purchasing your ancestral lands and keeping them in the family. I think the property is being offered at a bargain price and I am tempted to buy it myself, but I find myself a trifle overextended at the moment."

Alex was shocked by what he was hearing and finding it difficult to believe a man that he felt had the persona of a snake oil salesman. "That's quite a story, Mr. Lardsome, but how can I be sure that that Leonard family is the same as my great grandmother's?"

Lardsome pushed his neat pile of papers across the table and then watched as Alex gave them a quick inspection.

Shit, that's even a copy of my great grandparents' wedding certificate. 'Busybody' hardly describes this nosy asshole!

"It's all there, Alex. Do you mind if I call you Alex? What do you say? I think this is an opportunity not to be missed."

Lardsome looked left and right as if checking for eavesdroppers, then leaned as far forward across the table as his bulk permitted. "There is some further information you should bear in mind: good news and bad news concerning your cousin. The bad news is that Mister Leonard has terminal cancer and is spending his last days in a palliative care ward at the Veterans' Hospital in Halifax. The good news, at least for you, Alex, is that he has no heirs."

Lardsome flashed a quick smile as if he had just brought home a clever punch line. "When I informed him that I had found you, he said, as a last wish, that he wanted the property to stay in the family. He is offering the land to you at a price greatly reduced from the one that initially sparked my interest. The new price, which I assume would provide for a suitable funeral for him, is so low that, should you purchase the property yourself, I would be in a position to buy the property from you while still assuring you a small profit from the transaction. So, you see, it would be a win/win situation for everybody concerned."

Alex shoved his cold cup of coffee aside, gathered up the papers and made to stand up. "I'll go over these documents and look into this matter more myself. If all this pans out, maybe, I'll contact you." *Not far off the mark: snake oil salesman for sure.*

"All right, Alex, but don't wait too long; time is of the essence—the doctor says your poor cousin only has days to live."

~

Alex, Nancy, Horst, Saul and the other two women sat at the long table in the larger tent. A stiff breeze was blowing, and the Leonard documents were spread out, held in place by stones. Alex, lifting and reading each item, was explaining the situation he had found himself in. "So, what do you think? Should I buy this useless two hundred acres and trust that fatso is going to live up to his promise and let me flip them to him, or forget the whole thing? I'm not even sure that the guy selling it *is* my cousin. What do you think, Saul?"

"This kind of puts me on the spot, Alex. My family is in the business of property speculation and acquisition and has been trying to get me involved for years. They don't understand that I don't want anything to do with it. But I guess it's in my blood, because I can't help analyzing the situation and deciding that you have been offered a good deal."

Alex looked around the table turning to Horst for further advice and assurance. "What do you think?"

"I guess I have a couple of questions. How are you going to make Lardsome keep his word and are you absolutely sure that this Leonard guy is really a blood relative of yours? I don't know how to secure Lardsome's offer, but do know how to confirm Leonard's claim? Don't forget, I'm in the business of checking DNA and I have the best lab in the province at my disposal."

~

"Here's the deal I'm offering, Nigel—I hope you don't mind me calling you Nigel. I'm told that five thousand dollars is a more than fair price for two hundred acres. I have decided that I will take the risk, but with two provisos. First, my agreement to sell you the property will come into effect only if no unforeseen situation emerges that indicates that you have not been forthcoming with your assessment of the situation. Legal concerns aside, since you think that I might have some moral obligation to Mr. Leonard, I will need a DNA test to confirm my relationship with him. I will make the arrangements for someone to go to the hospital and get a sample. You get his permission and I'll look after the rest. Shall I get my lawyer to draw up an agreement?" *Horst is going to love this assignment.*

"No, not to worry, there is no need for that. I'm sure we can trust each other. You'll have permission for the test by tomorrow, and then we can get on with this. I've already prepared the offer to purchase. It's ready for the lawyers."

Lardsome leaned forward and offered his hand. Alex took it reluctantly and they said their goodbyes.

~

The cleanup of the old blacksmith shop and its surrounds was beginning. Backhoes, bobcats and forklifts had appeared out of nowhere. Tow trucks were pulling wrecked vehicles out of the mud, hauling some away and positioning others where they could be hoisted onto waiting trucks and flatbeds. Heavily burdened transports were leaving, returning an hour or so later after they discharged their cargoes at nearby scrap yards, ready for the next loads. It was a bit of a free-for-all, with several local dealers vying for the rusty prizes.

Alex was worried that, with all the frantic activity, one of the heavy machines might hit and damage the building, so he stayed outside to keep a watchful eye. Any more damage and the old structure would be beyond redemption. Saul had volunteered to take care of the interior and supervise the crew of day workers Alex had recruited.

In addition to the two remaining hulks of old tractors and the bed and wheels of an ancient hay wagon, the inside of the building was packed to the rafters with seemingly-useless garbage. There was a tense moment when one of the tractors being winched out struck the door frame and had the whole building creaking and shuddering. Saul was quick to halt the operation before more damage could be done.

After the last tractor and the hay wagon deck had been carefully winched out through the big front door, Saul and his helpers set about removing the mountain of remaining items piece by piece. The crew members kept getting sidetracked with all the old bits, discussing the value of this and that until Saul found himself having to shout at them to get a move on. "Just throw the damned things into the bin. If you want any of the stuff, make yourself a pile down by the road and pick it up later."

The work progressed all day, with Alex managing the activity in the yard and only checking in with Saul when there was a lull outside.

By late afternoon the crew had removed everything in the building, except for a huge, tightly-packed, cone-shaped pile of musty tarps and fish nets in the middle of the floor. Four members of the crew were pulling at the edges of the topmost layers when suddenly, in a waft of dust, the covers gave way, exposing what had been concealed beneath them.

A shaft of light had made its way through a hole in the roof, illuminating the spot, and as the dust settled, Saul saw it: a huge anvil mounted on a heavy oak stump. He knew what it was, who must have owned it, and what it would mean to Alex.

Running outside he saw his friend seeing off the last of the truckers. "C'mere, Alex, follow me. You've got to see this!"

Alex followed reluctantly, expecting to be confronted with yet another problem item. But when he entered the darkened main room of the shop and was faced by the surreal vision of the anvil, still bathed in sunlight, he stopped in his tracks.

He stood dumbstruck for a moment. "Good Lord, Saul, do you suppose that's Ben Johnson's anvil?"

"Of course it is; who else's would it be? That was probably your great grandfather's most prized possession, and now it's yours. That lazy bastard Homer Leonard couldn't have known it was there, or he would have sold it long ago. I touched it when it was first exposed. Come over and touch it for yourself."

Alex followed Saul over and let him direct his hand onto the cold steel.

"Do you feel it, Alex?"

"Do I feel what, Saul?"

"The vibes, the same vibes you feel when you touch his tombstone on the mountain. He knows you're here and that you belong here. You must feel it. Tell me you feel it, Alex."

Alex appreciated the care and concern Saul had for the spirits of his ancestors, but did not really believe in their actual ghostly presence. However, he felt obliged to humour his friend with an answer that wouldn't offend his occult leanings.

When he looked around the building, thinking of what he could do with the anvil, he was suddenly consumed with the notion that maybe at least a part of him did belong there, so it was easy to answer, "You might be right Saul, you might be right."

~

Alex and Saul were making a final inspection of the property around the shop when the Volkswagen pulled in and the rest of the family poured out. They had baskets and hampers of food.

Jack, who had spent the day up at the campsite on the mountain, immediately ran over to Alex and, after a frantic greeting, he and Alex joined the group. They all made their way into the interior of the shop. The women were immediately struck by the image of the anvil basking in a now-gentler column of evening light.

Inspiration struck, and Marina and Dawn went back to the van and retrieved four folding camp tables. They erected them around the stump and its anvil. Nancy sat Jimmy down on a blanket out of the way while she and Heather arranged the celebratory feast they had been preparing all day on the tables. They added the wild flowers they had collected on their way down the mountain.

Nancy then picked up Jimmy and, with him on her hip, moved over beside Alex and slipped her arm around behind him. "It looks wonderful, Alex, I think we should always keep it right here."

It was the first time she had ever said 'we' about them, and he liked the sound of it.

42: The Order of the Round Table

It was unanimous: everybody in the family agreed that the anvil and its stand should always remain in the centre of the floor of the blacksmith shop. It belonged. More than anything or anybody, it belonged in the centre of the large common-room-to-be. They planned to build a large round table around it, so it would always be part of the story of the building.

As far as the building itself, the first thing was to make it tight, starting with the roof. Alex took to the woods above the shop with the help of Saul and Horst, when he was free on weekends. With old Stanley stopping in to give him pointers about his newly-acquired chainsaw, he began to cut down and limb the handiest mature spruces. Stanley had said that taking those trees would kill two birds with one stone. In addition to providing the timber he needed, he would be clearing an old woods road and creating a direct line of sight up to the graveyard on the mountain.

Queenie had been an excellent choice for a yard horse—two trips down the mountain to where they had placed the portable mill and she knew her job and, as Saul soon learned, it was best to stand aside and let her get on with it herself. Alex would hook the logging dogs to the trunk and all Saul had to do down at the mill was wait till she arrived, unhook the log and send her back up for more.

The mill operator's hours were flexible, and that was just as well because, as they began stripping away the rusty roofing and the several layers of wood and asphalt shingles beneath it, they exposed the old roofing boards and many of them needed to be replaced. The boards weren't the standard size of today, and the replacement wood would have to be sawn to the same thickness of the 150-year-old planks.

When the roof had been stripped and most of the damaged areas repaired, Saul made an unusual design request, "This is the exact spot where the hole in the roof let the shaft of sun in when we discovered the anvil. If you think your budget will allow it, Alex, I think you should put a skylight here. Better still, one of those new fancy tunnel lights."

"As you know, my friend, money isn't really an issue with me, but what is your thinking?"

"Well, Rockefeller, I see that anvil and where it is placed as sort of a shrine, and if that skylight is positioned correctly, at certain times, on certain days, at certain times of the year a shaft of light like the one that beamed on that anvil will appear. We could even arrange ceremonies around it."

"You and your bloody ceremonies, Saul. That shaft

of light must be some powerful to levitate and place a three hundred pound anvil where it did, but I like the idea of the skylight, so your wish is my command."

Alex had had several copies of the photo of the old smithy, and passed them around to the family members. He wanted their suggestions regarding its restoration. They all agreed that they should try to change as little as possible.

The roof had posed the first problem. In the photo, the roof was covered with the traditional wooden shingles of the period, but the type of small mills that was used to produce them from a number of different local softwoods no longer existed. In any event, the first visit from the county building inspector, probably initiated by a jealous Nigel Lardsome, confirmed that wooden shingles of any sort would not be permitted.

Nancy was quick to suggest that, from a strictly visual perspective, many of the newer asphalt shingles could create much the same look. Alex was quietly pleased with what he sensed was her increasingly proprietary interest in the project and, out loud, agreed with her idea.

Days became weeks as, piece by piece, they repaired, replaced and restored almost every inch of the exterior of the old forge. They replaced decayed old spruce shingles with costly cedar imports, replicating as closely as they could the old designs seen in the photo. Alex, aware of his limitations, had decided that, since he would shortly have to return to Toronto, he should pull out all the stops and hire the proper tradespeople for the jobs that were piling up.

The interior of the building was a special challenge. They left the beautiful old beams exposed, but in between them there was now insulation and gyprock. There was a new cement floor, trowelled and polished under the watchful eye of Saul, who cautioned the workmen to steer clear of the anvil.

There was a circular staircase that gave access to the second floor. It led up to a hallway with two small bedrooms over one half of the floor. But for a small bathroom, the other half was for the larger master bedroom.

Six weeks after the work began, they held a special house warming, inviting friends and family and many of the people who had participated in the construction. There was a cloudy start to the day, threatening rain by the time everybody arrived at the smithy.

Around the new table was one of Alex's treasured finds: twelve pressed-back chairs. Everyone had settled and Alex was mid-sentence in a greeting when, outside and above, the grey clouds parted and a golden shaft of light poured down through the skylight illuminating the old anvil nestled in its circle of flowers.

Everybody gasped and Saul looked over at Alex with an 'I told you so' look on his face.

~

For over two months Alex had been spending his days down at the smithy. It was all but finished. A few more tiles around the tub and shower stall in the second bathroom he had added as an afterthought at the back of the building, and everything would be complete.

The anvil and the round table sat prominently on the highly-polished cement floor that reflected the light from the glass-fronted stove they had installed where the old forge had been. The original chimney remained, with a new steel insert to bring it up to code.

With all the potential comfort at his disposal, Alex still made the trip up the mountain to the campsite every night to sleep with Nancy. The new, larger tent he had put up to make things more comfortable for Jimmy and the two of them was serving its purpose, but he hoped he could convince a reluctant Nancy to move down to share the little home they had created together. She still seemed content to continue to cook over an open fire pit rather than use the beautiful new kitchen.

At first Alex thought that she didn't want any further commitment to him; but then, after a tearful, tell-all confession in his arms, he realized that she was still very afraid. She couldn't bring herself to leave what had been her safe haven.

He asked her to contact Father Crosby to find out the status and location of Mark, and the priest had assured her that he was in good hands a safe distance way, but she still couldn't bring herself to take the chance and put herself and her son in what could be harm's way.

Alex had all but given up hope of convincing her otherwise until one evening when he arrived at the campsite. He found the place in turmoil. Everybody was upset and clustered around Nancy, who cradled a moaning Jimmy in her arms.

"Thank God you're here, Alex. Feel his forehead. Does it feel hot to you?"

"We all felt him." one of the women said. "He does feel hot."

Alex reached through the folds of the blanket around Jimmy, touched his forehead and gently lifted him out of Nancy's arms, "Get you things together, Nan; we're going to the hospital."

She sat mutely beside him on the seat of the old truck, with Jimmy on her lap, as they raced down the slope towards Middleton. Ignoring the signs in the hospital's parking lot, Alex headed directly to the closest spot to the main entrance, jumped out of the truck and ran around to the passenger door. Taking Jimmy from her arms, he set off at a run for emergency.

Nancy had just caught up to him when he reached the triage nurse, who didn't seem to be too concerned. Alex heard her whisper out of the corner of her mouth to another nurse, "Just another first time mother with a croupy kid—no need to disturb the doctor."

Alex lost it. "What the hell are you saying? You don't know what the problem is. You haven't even taken Jimmy's temperature. You call a doctor and you call one now or by god I'll...I'll...I'll—"

"Okay, Sonny, don't get your knickers in a knot. Susan, would you please give Doctor Cruess a buzz?"

~

Nancy stood hand in hand with Alex while Dr. Cruess gently placed Jimmy on the examination table. As he took the boy's temperature and listened to his lungs under the watchful eye of the old nurse, Dr. Cruess was instinctively aware that what he really was addressing was the anxiety of a worried father. "Nothing to worry about here, Mr. Johnson, it's just a little cough and a bit of the croup."

And then to smooth the waters, he added, "I understand why you are so concerned about your son. You've got to be careful with stuff like this. Never know when a case of meningitis is going to pop up, but you and your wife can stop worrying on that score."

Nancy and Alex looked at each other quizzically, but neither of them corrected the doctor's mistake.

Equipped with prescriptions and the haughtily-proffered advice of the smug nurse, they bundled up Jimmy and headed back to the truck. The nearby pharmacy was quick to provide what they needed, and Alex could see that Nancy was no longer feeling so desperate.

But before he put his foot down on the accelerator for the trip back home, he put his foot down on a more important matter. "We're not taking this little guy back up to that soggy tent. We're going straight to the smithy and you are going to get used to staying there."

There was silent acquiescence from the passenger seat.

Shit, shit shit! That Ikea crib is still sitting in its box upstairs. I should have put it together when it came the other day.

Alex swung the door to the smithy open and stepped aside to let Nancy enter. "You guys settle down here for a moment while I go up and make the bed. I'm afraid there isn't a proper place for Jimmy yet. Would you mind Jimmy sleeping with us for tonight? That way we can keep a close eye on him."

Alex knew full well that Nancy wouldn't object. Jimmy had spent every other night in bed with them. He'd starting crawling out of his wooden box crib in the middle of the night, and would squeeze in between them and Jack.

Bed made, he called down to Nancy, "Be careful of those bloody steps. Circular staircases look good but they aren't all that practical."

Alex knew that when he had Nancy safely up the stairs he had one last uncomfortable hurtle to overcome. He hurried along the hallway that led to what he preferred to call the master bedroom at the front of the building, but paused before entering.

"I hope you're ready for this, Nan. I just finished it today."

Nancy edged around him and peered into the

room. "What the hell? What is that?"

"I know I should have discussed this with you… but it's something I have always wanted. We can take it down if you don't like it."

Suspended from four strong chains anchored in the exposed beams of the rafters, a heavy wooden frame enclosed a king-sized box spring and mattress. "It's a swinging bed. I got the idea from the sort of thing they use on ships."

Nancy began to laugh. She moved forward, placed Jimmy on the bed and gave it a bit of a push to send it moving. Jimmy, even in his groggy state, responded instantly with a happy giggle.

"So you really mean it to be simply a swinging bed and not a swinger's bed?"

"That thought never occurred to me," Alex responded with mock annoyance.

The following day they assembled the crib, placing it a safe distance from the swinging bed in case any extra movement set it on a dangerous spiral.

The one major plus about the bed was that Jack refused to join them. He had made his one and only frantic leap onto it but immediately abandoned ship when it flew forward and struck the wall, sending him flying. He preferred to spend his nights under Jimmy's crib, out of range of the pendulous swing.

Alex and Nancy filled the back of the old truck with the few things that Nancy had at the camp and brought them down to their new home. They had made their move.

43: Agree to disagree

Alex and Saul were sitting at the round table in the now nearly-totally refurbished blacksmith shop when they heard Nigel Lardsome's car arrive. He was right on time for their meeting. But this was not going to be the meeting Mr. Lardsome was expecting.

Alex had gone ahead with the purchase of the large Leonard property on North Mountain from his supposed very distant relative. Lardsome had told him that the cousin wouldn't sell the property to him, even though he had told him he planned to build a house for himself on the old site. The old fellow must have spotted the ruse and insisted he would only sell it to Alex, his relative, and as soon as possible. He had debts to settle before he died.

Alex had asked his friend Horst to confirm his relationship with the dying man, and a DNA test confirmed that they were indeed related. Alex had then agreed, with the provisos that he would buy and then flip the property into Lardsome's name, charging only the cost of his own legal expenses in addition to the original purchase price, but only if no undisclosed circumstances came to light before the transfer.

Nigel Lardsome came swaggering through the front door, all smiles and full of bravado, with a sheaf of official papers clutched in his hand.

"Grab a chair, Mr. Lardsome. I hope you don't mind that I've invited Mr. Levy to join us."

"Not at all, not at all. The more the merrier, I always say." Then, thumping the papers down on the table, he continued, "Here, feast your eyes on this. Good news—you are about to receive three times the amount you paid for the property."

Alex read the first page of the transfer of deed and passed it over to Saul, who casually flipped a couple of pages of the agreement and passed it back to Alex.

"I don't see your name on this deed application. It says here that the purchaser is a company called Amalgamated Quarry Systems, an American outfit. Would you care to explain, Mr. Lardsome?"

"Just a matter of practicality, Mr. Johnson. Why go to the trouble of two transfers and involve God only knows how many lawyers? I assure you that I will be well compensated and you can see in front of you the handsome sum you are about to receive."

"I'll be honest with you, Nigel, I hope you don't mind me calling you Nigel, but the name on the application for transfer of deed is not a surprise to me or my associate, Mr. Levy. It seems, however, that you have not been honest with me. I took the opportunity to go up and have a look at the property the other day, and brought Mr. Levy along. It was at his suggestion. He cautioned that it was never good to buy a pig in a poke, even if you were just planning to flip it.

He knows all about this stuff. Anyway, we were both surprised to come across a survey company busy establishing the boundaries. This was happening without my permission and I questioned the surveyor whether it was standard procedure in Nova Scotia for a company like his just to barge in on private property. He dodged the question but offered the name of the company that was employing him. You guessed it, the same name that's on this document."

Alex let a tense pause build, then said, "I am not prepared to sell my property to Amalgamated Quarry Systems, which intends to turn a beautiful property into a pitted moonscape. I'm not, at this point, prepared to sell it to anyone. And that includes you, Nigel."

Lardsome opened his mouth, shut it, then opened it again. But before he could speak, Alex said, "In an effort to be fair and honest, something that you don't seem to comprehend, I have prepared a cheque as a suitable finder's fee."

"But...but—"

"No buts about it. Take these papers and this cheque, if you want it, and get out of here!"

Lardsome silently pulled the papers from the table, picked up the cheque, gave it a quick look before cramming it in his pocket, and headed toward the door. He paused there and turned back with a malicious look on his face and pulled a folded paper from an inner pocket and threw it on the floor.

"Read that and weep, jackass."

After Lardsome had slammed the door, Saul got

up slowly, picked up the discarded paper, and brought it over to the table. Together, he and Alex read the clear longhand notation.

> Excerpt from ledger # 1890 A-27
> Middleton Baptist Church
> (Copy from page 30 of Church records)
> Penned by Reverend Angus McKay
>
>
> Wednesday July 27,1890
> 11.00 am
> Chaired a meeting of the Ladies Auxiliary. Confirmed arrangements for the annual Fund Raiser and appointed Miss Joyce Waverly as Assistant Sunday School Teacher.
> 12.00 PM
> Adjourned for lunch.
> 12.30 pm
> Met with parishioner Mrs. Mary Neilly, at her request for a private meeting. Mrs. Neilly apprised me of a serious situation that needed my immediate attention. A young woman obviously in the family way had appeared at a neighbour of hers, the blacksmith, Ben Johnson. It is widely rumoured that the father of the young woman's soon to arrive child was one or more of her own brothers.
> I suggested that the place for her would be the County Poor Farm but Mrs. Neilly

said that that solution had been proposed to Mr. Johnson and dismissed out of hand.

At Mrs. Neilly's insistence I reluctantly consented to perform a wedding that was mutually agreed upon by both participants: Ben Johnson, age 53, and Lilly Leonard, age 15.

This was not the first request of this kind that I have been presented with and am convinced that speed and discretion are the best way to serve the Lord in these matters.

3.00 pm

The Neillys picked me up at the church and provided transportation to the home of Benjamin Johnson.

4.00 pm

Performed nuptials and required the usual fee for the church coffers but Mr. Johnson added a substantial bonus and a most appreciated offer to keep the mare I use to pull the buggy for my visits to parishioners shod for as long as I wished.

It was a generous offer that set me wondering about the man's real motives and intentions.

5.00 pm

I declined any offer of refreshment and Mr. Neilly drove me back to town. Mrs.

Neilly remained with the newlyweds and prepared a repast for the couple.

    6.00 pm

    Choir practice in the church.

44: The church record

Nancy was upstairs, putting Jimmy down for his afternoon nap, when she heard Lardsome's car pulling up in front of the smithy. She might have gone down to join Alex and Saul for the meeting that she knew wouldn't go well for the horrid man, but she chose to forgo the pleasure. She stayed out of sight, listening at the top of the stairs. She heard every word of the exchange until a strange silence ensued after Lardsome took his leave.

She wasn't able to make out the whispered exchanges between Alex and Saul as they sat side by side, heads together quietly reading over something.

"What's the buzz, boys?" she asked cheerfully as she descended the stairs.

Both men had troubled looks on their faces.

"C'mon guys, what's going on? I thought you really ripped him."

At that Saul got to his feet. He looked apologetically at her then back at Alex with a look that said, *I think I better leave you on your own with this one, buddy.* Then he went to the door.

Alex looked up at her with tears in his eyes. "Come and sit with me, Nan. I need you to read this."

Nancy sat down and read the ancient paper, going over it several times. After a long pause, she turned to Alex. "What is this? What does it mean?"

Alex leaned over and put his arm around her and drew her closer. "This is a church record that this minister, a Reverend McKay, filled out on the day that my great grandfather and great grandmother got married. It's perfectly clear that Ben Johnson was not my real grandfather. I already knew that, but what that jerk Lardsome was delighting in letting me know was that the father of my grandfather, Dan Johnson, was one of my great grandmother's brothers. Nancy, that's what the minister was disclosing— a case of incest."

"But that was a long time ago. A lot of DNA has gone under the bridge since then. A little shocking, but jeez, why the tears?"

"It's a long story, my sweet, and you already know a lot of it. I think my grandfather wanted me to bring his ashes here because he felt guilty that he'd abandoned the place. I think this record explains why he never wanted to return. He never came out and said anything about it, but now I think he must have known and spent his whole life troubled about how it might affect his children, and maybe even their children."

"Meaning you, Alex?"

"Yes, meaning me." He took her hand in his and looked into her eyes. "And maybe more than just me. Who knows where this sort of thing ends?"

"I think you're worrying about nothing. In the first

place, that clever old prick Lardsome might have forged this. And even if it's true, it happened so long ago it couldn't possibly affect you. I think you should wait until Horst gets back from the city and talk to him. He knows all about this stuff."

45: The meeting

The weekend and Horst's return to the Valley could not have come too soon for Alex. He had almost worn the copy of the church record out, unfolding, folding it, and sharing it with everybody in the camping family, who he now thought of as family.

Everybody knew that Horst would have the final word on the matter, but he had declined to broach the subject over the phone, choosing rather to share his words of wisdom at what would look like a formal gathering around the table. This occasion had been at the behest of Saul, who everybody knew could not resist the opportunity for a ceremony of any kind.

When Horst arrived, he joined the group who were sitting in silent anticipation. Saul had insisted that he take what was designated as the seat of honour. Alex had willingly deferred the chairmanship to Saul—he just wanted to get on with it.

Saul picked up the ancient, long-handled hammer that they had discovered in a wall cavity during the renovation, reached forward, and gently tapped the anvil. "I call this meeting to order."

Everyone suppressed smirks and maintained

their composure.

Brandishing the now worn and dog-eared church record, he continued, "Since this document has caused our Brother Alex such anxiety and concern, I move that we call on Brother Horst to address this meeting and venture an opinion. Would anyone care to second the motion?"

There was a long pause and everybody began to look quizzically at each other.

"I said, would anybody like to second the motion!"

Alex lifted off his chair, "Oh for god's sake, Saul. Yes, I'll second it. Can we please get on with this?"

Looking slightly hurt, he replied, "Okay, I yield the floor to Brother Horst."

Horst was surprised and amused by the unexpected formality of the meeting, but decided not to indulge Saul anymore and cut right to the chase.

"My friend Alex and the lovely Nancy have been worrying unnecessarily for the better part of a week over the contents of that old church record. Whether the information it apparently discloses is true, we have no way of verifying. More importantly, we have no need to, because we have current, scientifically-verified evidence that most probably refutes it. I am going to have to get a little technical now so you will have to bear with me."

Horst looked around to confirm he had everyone's attention. "Alex seems to be concerned that, if the information in the record is correct, it might somehow have implications for him. He wonders if some of the traits that may have been embedded in his great grandmother's genome might still be present and dangerous. I can ease his mind in two ways. First, in the sample of his DNA that he provided some time ago, there was no sign of homozygosity."

Alex looked confused. "What the hell does that mean?"

"Not to be worried. It's just a technical term. People who are the result of incest have identical versions of a particular gene in their DNA. You, my friend, have no evidence of anything like that in your sample. If anything, the diverse nature of the contributions in your genome suggests something that contradicts the claim in that record."

"Whew... that's good news!"

"Yes, good news for you, Alex, but, unfortunately, that doesn't let your grandfather off the hook. I am now more determined than ever to get Professor Martin to have a good look at Dan Johnson's DNA sample from The Valour Project. He seemed unaccountably interested in your sample and said, when he had more time, he would like to explore the matter further. This will be very timely, because the UK Biobank is currently doing a study of possible incidents of incest, using a database of 450,000 participants. I'm sure the Professor could get them to slip your grandfather's sample into the batch. I would need your written permission. Do you really want to pursue this?"

At that a slender shaft of light made its way down from the skylight and lit up a portion of the anvil.

After letting the silence draw out to an almost-unbearable length, Horst leaned forward and spoke gently. "Alex, I asked you, do you want me to pursue this? Do you want to think this over?"

"I've been thinking this over too much already. Lay on, MacDuff!"

46: What we're going to do

Alex stored the copy of the church record at the back of a file of documents his new lifestyle was accumulating and tried to push what it revealed to the back of his mind. He wasn't having much success, particularly at night.

Despite Horst's comforting words at the family meeting, he was having frequent nightmares full of encounters with hideous, deformed figures moving toward him out of a mist, offering their hands, chuckling and inviting him to join them.

He shouldn't have researched the effects of inbreeding after Lardsome's revelation, because now he was preoccupied with what he was reading during the day and haunted by it at night: cleft palate, limb malformation, blindness, congenital heart disease, neonatal diabetes—the list went on. Horst provided little comfort when he said that the literature suggested that most of the problems might only manifest themselves in first-generation incest situations.

Why did he have to emphasize the word <u>*might*</u>, *anyway? Dan Johnson was first generation and I'm sure he spent his whole life worrying about what might be in store for him and his offspring. Thank god Nancy is here to keep me sane.*

When Alex came down for breakfast one morning following one of his restless nights and found Nancy sitting at the round table, quietly crying, he was consumed with guilt and bending down, put his arms around her. "Oh God, I'm sorry, Nan. I've been putting too much on your shoulders. Did you get any sleep? Did I wake up Jimmy with my yelling?"

"No, Alex, it's not that. It's...it's—"

"What is it, Nan, please tell me."

There was a long pause.

"I'm pregnant, Alex, and I don't know what to do. I don't know what to do."

Alex pulled her in tighter to him and kissed her forehead, then remained silent for a moment. Then he whispered softly in her ear, "I'll tell you what you are going to do. You're going to marry me. I know you're already married, but that won't be forever. And when you get free we are going to get married. Don't argue—I've made up mind!"

"You arrogant bastard. What makes you think I would marry you? I haven't even said that I love you."

"Well, I kind got the notion by the way you've been acting up on that swinging bed, and I sure as hell know that I have fallen in love with you and that little Jimmy. So what's it going to be?"

He kissed her full on her lips and they both knew that a spoken answer was not necessary.

47: Give it a try

Nancy went upstairs to get Jimmy while Alex gave Jack his breakfast.

"Here, have a little extra, you greedy bugger. I guess this should be a bit of a celebration—you just acquired a family!"

Alex had Jimmy's special seat in place when Nancy arrived with him and, after securing the boy with the safety belt, he went over to the kitchen counter, returned with the bunny bowl full of Jimmy's favourite cereal. While Nancy gave him the first spoonfuls, Alex got mugs of coffee for her and himself, and the three of them settled in.

"This is the way I see it, Nan. We'll all head back to Toronto as soon as you can get yourself ready. I've got a fully-furnished, ready-to-go house waiting for us, so there's no need to delay. We'll keep this place as a summer home and come here as often as you want."

"Whoa! Settle down, boyo! First off, I didn't say… out loud at least, that I would marry you and I have no desire to live in a big city."

"Oh c'mon, Nan, you'll love it—lots to do and see up there."

"I'm a country girl from Saskatchewan. I don't think I could stand it. I don't think the city would be a good environment for Jimmy or this little life that's starting in me. And what about Jack and Queenie? Are you going to leave them behind?"

"I've thought about that. There's no way I'm going to leave behind a dog that probably saved my life, and I know I can arrange to board Queenie at the stables I used to work at. There's always been a German Shepherd at my grandfather's house and I can exercise the pair of them the same way Gramps used to. C'mon, Nan, at least say you'll give it a try."

~

Just over three months after Nancy told Alex she was pregnant, they were on the plane heading back to Nova Scotia. Jimmy was with them and Jack was enduring a crate in the cargo hold. Two weeks in Toronto were more than enough to convince them that they didn't belong there.

Nancy had been so proud of Alex when he had insisted that Saul and the rest of his family move into the old shop. They couldn't survive the winter in their tents on the mountain, and they would be safe, warm and secure in the restored building. Alex knew they would treasure and protect it the way they treated the old graveyard.

Now here they were, coming back to where he had started. In Toronto they had arrived after their three-hour flight west, kid and dog in tow, and headed out to his grandfather's home in Parkdale. The place smelt a little mustier than Alex had remembered, but everything else was as he had left it.

He immediately set out in his rented car to purchase a crib, then spent hours going through the IKEA puzzle again. When it was finished, longing for his little bed in the blacksmith's shop, Jimmy would have nothing to do with it and opted instead to sleep between the couple in Gramps' old mahogany four poster.

Jack wasn't impressed with his new home either, when he realized the new restrictions imposed on him. Dan's old Jack might have been content with a regular walk on a leash and an occasional romp in the park, but the new Jack missed his time roaming in the woods, hunting rabbits on his own or seeking romantic liaisons with female dogs in the area.

More than anything else, it was the general hubbub of the city that got to them all. Constant traffic and huge crowds everywhere. They had grown used to the peace of their Valley.

On their tenth day of living their new life, Alex came home from his interview at police headquarters, bringing what he thought was going to be good news. He had been assured that he would be welcomed on the Mounted Unit. All he had to do was submit a formal application. He found Nancy sitting at the kitchen table with tears in eyes.

"I don't think I can do this....I can't...you stay, but... but—"

"What happened? What's going on?"

"I tried the subway, like you suggested, today. A man ran up to me and ripped my purse from me. Jimmy fell down on the deck."

"Is he hurt? Is Jimmy hurt?"

"He's all right; he's fine—just a little bruised. But I don't know what to do. What should I do, Alex?"

After a long pause, Alex said, "I've always loved this place. I think it's because it was like a sort of time capsule. Nothing about it ever changed since my grandfather bought it in 1950. All the furniture's just the way he and my grandmother had it when they moved in. I always felt safe and secure here. But I guess I have been fooling myself."

"About what?"

"It's still 1950 in here. But if you step out the door, it's a different world, not a very nice one. I remember Gramps telling me that the gang that troubled the city the most was called the Beanery Gang. I can't imagine why they would come up with a name like that. They didn't have guns like the gangs today. Gramps just carried a WWI Webley pistol—I think it's still around here somewhere. He and his horse were part of a posse that hunted down the Boyd gang, whoever they were, when they escaped from the Don Jail. I'm not saying it wasn't bad back then. They actually hung two cop killers there in Gramps' time. Gramps knew the policeman they killed. So, it could be bad back then but nothing like today."

Alex got up and looked out the nearest window at houses and houses, on to the horizon. He could almost feel the pulse of too much activity, like the sound of a badly-balanced clothes dryer.

"I've had enough of it, too. Reading the local head-lines every day just about makes me sick. I don't want to put our lives in jeopardy each time we go out the door. I want the safety and quiet of the Valley for all of us, too. So I totally agree with you, let's get out of here pronto."

It wasn't quite that simple. Closing up the house, packing up all the things Alex cherished and the things Nancy treasured, was a big job. Neither of them had much love for the heavy, dark Victorian furniture that filled the place, so Alex consigned it to an auction firm. He was beyond glad that they had waited on transporting Queenie from Nova Scotia.

Five days after they made their decision, they watched the last of the furniture head out the door for the auction house, the movers loaded up their boxes and crates, and the rental agent picked up the house keys.

That evening they were on the plane, headed back east.

48: Surprises all around

Alex had no way of getting in touch with Saul to let him know that they were on the way. It would have to be a surprise for his family.

It turned out to be more of a surprise for Alex and Nancy. After all the hoots and hugs, and the tea was poured, Saul had some unexpected news for them. Almost all of the family members had packed up their bags and were preparing to move on.

Saul explained, "As you know, I am an American citizen and for the most part a proud American citizen, but something happened some time back that made me feel ashamed of my country and I felt obliged to turn away from it. I am, as most people term it, a draft dodger. Who wanted to go to Vietnam? Because of that I haven't seen my family for years. In 1977 they pardoned people who for good reasons had avoided the draft. I thought I was home free and would be able to see my family again. I was almost ready to cross the border. It was lucky that I didn't because, as it turned out, obtaining a pardon for me would have been complicated. I had spent a couple of hours in a recruiting office and signed some documents that technically made me a Service member. I wasn't just a draft dodger. I was classified as a deserter."

Everybody said "Oooh," and Saul grinned.

"I could still be pardoned, but my family's lawyers say it would be a long process, very complicated. It has taken six years to be exact, but last week they approved my pardon. My mother is ecstatic about the news. My father is very ill and I'm needed there immediately. Marina and I have rented a car and we're off to the States tomorrow."

"Tomorrow!" Alex said. "So no time to plan a farewell party."

Saul shrugged. "I've never been big on long goodbyes. But there's further good news. We all knew there was something going on between Horst and Heather. Well, they have decided to get married and will be shipping out to Germany. Dawn has decided that she could use some time on her own and is going into Halifax to stay with an old school mate."

"Dawn, how will you get there?" Nancy asked.

"Horst and Heather are taking the shuttle to the airport," she said. "So I inherit the van."

"So there you have it," Saul said. "You'll have the place all to yourselves, but you're not forever. Horst is making plans for our annual reunions—if that's all right with you."

Three men, a child, four pregnant women, and a dog moved forward into a very complex hug.

49: Reunions

As good as his word, Horst set about organizing the family's first annual reunion. It was to be in the fall of 1993. He thought, and everybody agreed, that their little Eden was at its best when the fall leaves were in their colourful profusion. By then all of the expected offspring would be well established and able to travel.

There was a bit of concern that the tents, still safe and ready to be put up again back at the campsite, might not be adequate for the weather, but Alex and Nancy assured everyone that it would not be an issue. They had a surprise in store for them.

It was Nancy's idea. The two of them had been standing on the road looking back at the restored blacksmith shop. Alex had the old picture in his hand, comparing it to the way it looked in 1902.

"Have a look, Nan. It looks just about the way it used to. What do you think?"

She took the photo and held it a distance from her to create the proper perspective. Then she said, "It looks great, but it would look even better if the house and barn behind it in the photo were still there."

She was right. He wished that he had thought of it himself, but she was right. They looked at each other and simultaneously headed back into the shop to dig out paper and pencil.

They sat at the kitchen table, loaded with fresh cups of coffee, studying the photo while the two children played with a tolerant dog. Forgetting to congratulate Nancy for what he now thought was a fabulous idea, Alex was first to broach the subject.

"We can probably almost duplicate this scene. No problem positioning the house and barn, because the rock foundations for all the old buildings are still in there, filled in and buried but still in place. We could dig them out and fix up the walls."

"That would be wonderful, Alex. It's just too bad we don't know what the interior looked like."

"All the better. You're always going on about how wonderful those open concept homes in your magazines look. It will take a bit of clever engineering, but we could do that."

"Do you really think we could? I'd love that!"

"I don't *think* we can. I *know* we can. And if I get started right away, we might get one of the buildings closed in this year. I'll start with the house."

Alex, using all the skills he had learned at his grandfather's side, had done all the carpentry work on the restoration of the old blacksmith shop and was more than eager to tackle something a little more challenging.

He might have contracted someone with a backhoe to dig out the house basement, but he wanted to preserve the rockwork in the walls as much as possible, so decide to dig it out with pick and shovel. He had second thoughts about this decision when he realized that there was still a bit of frost in the ground.

It was painstaking work, helped a little by using Queenie and a scoop improvised out of an old car hood. The old horse stood patiently as Alex loaded shovelful after shovelful of half-frozen dirt, junk metal, and bits of old tin. Then he and Queenie hauled the load up out of the foundation.

Ten days later Nancy stood with Lucie on her hip and Jimmy's hand in hers, at Alex's side, looking down into what would become the basement of their new home.

"The stones look well laid," Alex said, "but I think I'll form up around inside them and pour a new concrete wall. We'll need a nice smooth cement floor as well."

"Won't that cost a lot of money?"

"Damn the cost, girl. The way Saul has been making our investments grow, it'll be just a drop in the bucket."

"Whatever you say, Rockefeller, I've got to get back to the laundry."

In ten days, the forms were up, the cement poured and he felt they were well on their way. He had assembled far too many saw logs when he was working on the blacksmith shop and was thinking he would be able to use the lumber from them for a good portion of the house.

That's when the building inspector arrived.

"You can use that lumber from those logs, Mr. Johnson, but every stick of it will have to be graded, kiln dried and stamped. And I suggest you come down to the county office and get a thing we call a building permit. *And* you're going to have to supply a set of plans to get it!"

Two weeks later, with plans provided by a local architect in hand, it was off to the mill in Middleton with the logs. With luck, he would have it all back in about a month, ready for building.

In the meantime he bought some lumber to make a start, but he still felt that at least some of the new house should have originated from their own trees.

It wouldn't be until late that fall, during an early snow fall, that the whole family, including one dog, was able to stand inside, out of the weather, in the unfinished shell of their new home. They felt ready now to greet their dear friends and all the babies.

The much-anticipated day arrived and everybody was astonished by the sight of the almost-finished exterior of a house remarkably similar to the one they remembered from the old photo.

"Oh, look!" someone said. "You can see right up to that lookout place above our campground. It makes there and here feel really connected."

After having a good look around inside the house and hearing all the plans Alex and Nancy had for it, they moved on to the shop. Soon the round table at the centre of the smithy was cluttered with piles of diapers, rows of baby bottles, boxes of cereal, baby food, and all the paraphernalia related to travelling with infants.

They all talked and laughed at once, passing babies around and getting caught up with each other's lives. Alex joked that they better be careful or babies would end up with the wrong parents. One by one the babes were put down and to everyone's amazement, actually fell asleep.

In hushed tones, they continued to chat, commenting mainly on the sad state the world seemed to be in. Horst led with, "Isn't it awful about the space shuttle exploding and killing all the astronauts aboard?"

Saul said, "Tell me about it. Somebody tried to blow up The World Trade Center, and that's right in my backyard. I've got clients who have offices in those towers. I couldn't get back here fast enough to leave all that sort of stuff behind."

They all agreed that this place, and the campsite on the mountain above them, was a special sanctuary, a place where they were sure the problems of the outside world would not be able to penetrate.

Over the years, this prediction seemed to be holding true. As the seasons changed, days became weeks, weeks became months and months blended into years like the flickering calendar pages in an old movie. Their annual reunions became their marker in time as children grew, and life moved on and inflicted its mundane drama on their lives.

But all them faithfully returned each year and tried for a short time to relive their youthful dream of a Utopia.

Some of the dates of annual gatherings stood out above others.

In 2003, Saul opened the proceedings with, "Did you folks up here get the news about U.S. forces seizing control of Baghdad? I guess that ends the regime of that bastard, Saddam Hussein. His hometown of Tikrit has even fallen to U.S. forces—"

Saul stopped short. He could see that what he was saying was upsetting Nancy. "Christ! What was I thinking? The Iraq war is the last thing you need to be reminded of."

He paused for a long time, embarrassed and not knowing how to continue. Suddenly inspired, he said, "You know what? I might be wrong but I think the reason we all want to come back to our Eden is to forget all the crap that surrounds us when we're not here among our real friends." Saul picked up the long-handled hammer and struck the old anvil.

With the clang still ringing, he began again. "I move that in the future, whenever we meet here, we take only a short time to chew on all the news from *out there* and then, at the fall of this hammer, we never speak of it again while we are here."

He could have asked, "All in favour" but he could tell by the looks on their faces that that was not necessary.

And so the yearly ritual, and something they called the annual gong show, began, a brief opportunity to get rid of the baggage they brought from the outside world and then speak no more of it.

At the opening ceremony around the table in 2004, Alex took the gavel and began to speak about the run-ins he had had with their old nemesis, Homer Leonard. It had happened several times, always at night and always so fast that it was impossible to identify the dark figure, dressed in a hoodie, speeding down the road in front of the blacksmith shop on an old ATV.

There was often traffic passing by their home, and Jack had grown accustomed to it, but his reaction was different whenever he sensed the approach of the four-wheeler and its ghostly rider. He would start barking and snarling long before anyone else could hear it, then go berserk while it passed by. Jack would continue that uncharacteristic behaviour until the last sounds of the rattly old motor faded away in the distance.

Other neighbours had witnessed the noisy apparition and there was much speculation as to who it might be. Whoever it was, Jack had sensed something very wrong and dangerous about their mysterious passerby, and Alex had a great respect for the old dog's intuition.

On the other hand, Nancy was constantly concerned that, no matter how improbable it might be, somehow, someway, Mark would find his way back and fulfill his promise to kill Jimmy and her. She kept her concerns to herself but decided to call Father Crosby to make sure her crazy, estranged husband was safely locked away before leaning on Alex.

When she learned that the priest was away on a

retreat and couldn't be reached, her anxiety reached a new level. Even though she confided in Alex, she became inconsolable.

Alex suggested that he check with the authorities himself, but Nancy considered herself still in hiding and would have none of it. When he suggested that he lie in wait for the man he jokingly referred to as the Headless Horseman, she made him swear not to.

The answer as to who it was and why he was there came several days later, and not at night but in broad daylight. Alex, Nancy and the children were at the spring, collecting some of the water that they had developed a liking for way back in the first days of camping with Saul and the group. Nancy had Jack on the leash that they used only when he might be tempted to dart out into traffic if a rabbit or squirrel happened by.

Nancy felt the leash tighten, and then Jack started barking and trying to lunge away from her. The ATV skidded to a halt on the gravel on the shoulder of the road, barring the path that led from the spring to their car. The driver flung himself off the seat, pulled back his hood, and started moving menacingly toward them.

It was Homer Leonard, and he was mad and out of control. "You stole my property and jumped me from behind and got me landed in prison. I've been waiting for this chance to get you. Now I'm going to kick the shit out of you."

Alex turned quickly to Nancy and said, "Don't let Jack loose!" and to the dog, "Stay!"

Then he moved forward to confront the big man. He stopped a few feet short of his assailant and ducked the first wild punches directed at him.

Homer, drooling spit and tobacco juice, incensed further, growled, "Stand still, ya bastard. You can't get away. I'm going to fuckin' murder you."

Alex stepped back and threw his hands up in surrender. "There's nothing I can do, Homer." Then he pointed behind over the man's shoulder. "But that fellow in the uniform might have something to say about it."

Homer turned to look, giving Alex time to wind up and deliver a knockout punch. Looking skyward, he whispered "Thanks, again, Gramps."

He motioned to Nancy, who had already called 911 for help. The two of them gathered up the children and, along with Jack, stepped past Homer's motionless body. Jack took the keys out of the ATV, then they got in their car and drove a short distance away to wait for the police to arrive.

It wasn't long before an RCMP cruiser appeared, to find Homer on his feet again, searching frantically for his keys.

It meant more statements and court time for Alex and Nancy, but in the end Homer Leonard went back to Dorchester Prison for an extended stay and life at the base of the mountain resumed its peaceful rhythm.

When the family met for their reunion in 2005, Heather, who previously attended the reunions as a single mother with her little Tessa, had a surprise for the assembly. A tall, beautiful, dark-haired woman in her forties sat close beside Heather, who said, "This is Lisa. She's the friend I've been telling you about."

Saul, ever the self-appointed chair of all meetings, rose to give a formal greeting, but was cut short when Heather and Lisa thrust their left hands forward to display matching diamond engagement rings and gold wedding bands.

Everybody leaned in for a closer look as Saul sat down with a surprised look on his face and Heather resumed their story. "Lisa and I want you to know the good news. Obviously Lisa is no longer just my girlfriend. Two weeks ago a cruise ship called The Norwegian Dawn pulled into Halifax. It was stirring up quite a kerfuffle. Rosie O'Donnell had brought along ten same sex couples who wanted to take advantage of the recent Supreme Court's ruling. It was too good an opportunity to miss, so we stalked Rosie for two days until she agreed to include us in the group wedding."

Now recovered from the initial shock, Saul leapt to his feet, ran around the table, leaned in between the newlyweds and wrapped his arms around them, "I can't tell you how happy I am for both of you."

As the meeting adjourned and most of the women made a dash to check on the children and bring the food to the table, Lisa hung back and drew Horst aside. Looking around to be sure that they were out of earshot, she said, "I have something to ask you and I hope you won't be offended."

Horst sensed where this conversation might be

going and he wasn't sure how to handle it. "I'm really sorry if anything I have done...You know, Heather and me."

"No, no, no. Nothing of the kind." Lisa was blushing. "The thing is, Heather and I would love to have a big family. So...if you would be amenable, in the interest of genetic continuity, we would like you to... how I shall say it? To provide a similar service that gave us our little Tessa."

Horst, totally taken by surprise, replied, "I'm sure something could be arranged. I would have to clear it with Dawn, of course."

"The thing is, Horst, I hate to pressure you, but it turns out that the stars are in alignment, if you know what I mean, and the sooner we get on with this, the better."

As time went on, Heather and Lisa accumulated a family of four healthy children and over the years attended the family reunions to spend time with their doting parents as well as their loving biological father.

50: The pact

"I don't know why I never thought of this earlier, Alex. It's such an obvious solution."

Saul was standing at his usual position at the big table nervously twisting the long hammer handle.

"Okay, captain, what's on your mind?"

Everyone around the table turned and faced Saul with expectant looks on their faces.

"Well, it's like this. We all come here year after year trying to get back the wonderful feeling of freedom we once had, and we always lament that we can't bring back those days and find a way to return to this place permanently. We all know that that is almost impossible now and, if we are honest with ourselves, we know that it's never likely to happen. At least, that is what I had been thinking, until I realized that there is a way that we can actually make it happen. Not right away, but that doesn't really matter. We all know how welcoming those spirits of Alex's ancestors are up on the mountain, so this is what I propose."

He looked around dramatically, even though he already had everyone's attention. "You've all heard of living wills. You know, a legal document, other than the old standard will, that allows you to set out what you want done with your body when you pass. Well, I am suggesting that we all, when the time comes, opt for cremation and, if Alex is agreeable, stipulate that our ashes be spread up on the mountain with the other spirits. What do you say, Alex?"

Alex was tempted to laugh, but managed to suppress it. "Well, Saul, to be quite honest I've never thought about what I would want done you know... when. But now, I'm thinking that, if everybody else is in favour of it, it's a hell of an idea. I think it would work well with my plans. The house and barn will go to Nancy and the kids when I pack it in, but Nan and I have decided to donate the woodlots to the Nature Trust. We will add an encumbrance to the arrangement, so they will have to maintain the cemetery. I'm sure that that can be arranged."

"That's super, Alex. Now the rest of you: all in favour, raise your right hand."

There was no hesitation.

"That makes it unanimous. Just to make it legal, can everybody please bring a copy of your living will next year and...I know—we'll have a special ceremony."

Laughing, Alex retorted, "Can I at least request that, in the interest of decorum, and out of respect for our sagging bodies, we all keep our clothes on for this one?"

51: Make the effort

By the summer of 2007, Nancy's divorce was finalized and she and Alex decided to get married. They knew, with Saul's love of ceremony, they would not be able to simply tie the knot quietly and surprise everybody when they arrived for the reunion in a few weeks, so they asked Earle Smitherly, the registrar who had given them the marriage license, if he would preside at a small gathering back at the smithy.

It turned out he was also a justice of the peace but confessed that, although he was qualified to conduct marriages, he had never actually gone out and done one. He was close to retirement and the thought of doing something so outrageous was tempting. He phoned his wife and obtained her permission. He and his wife would be at the smithy at the appointed time.

At precisely 11 AM on Saturday, October 6, 2007, when everybody in the family had settled into their chairs, the door to the big common room swung open and Earle Smitherly and his wife entered.

Alex glanced at his watch, *Right on time.*

"Nancy and I have a surprise for all of you. Mr.

Smitherly here is a justice of the peace and he is here to marry us. His wife has kindly consented to act as a local witness."

Saul leapt to his feet. "You sneaky buggers! You should have let us know. I could have arranged a proper ceremony."

"That is precisely why I did not let you know in advance, my friend."

To which Saul, of course, had an answer. "Not to worry, we can all go up the mountain and celebrate afterwards. The folks up there will want to be part of this."

Earle Smitherly looked slightly confused. "Who are the folks on the mountain?"

"The spirits, the spirits!"

"Spirits? I'm not sure I've heard that family name around here before but my wife and I look forward to meeting them."

Alex said quickly, "I don't think that's a good idea, Mr. Smitherly. I think we better just stay here. The weather looks a bit iffy and we don't want you both to get caught up there in cloudburst." He was having visions of the family clustering naked around the tombstones with the Smitherlys, terrified, hot-footing it down the mountainside.

The ceremony went without a hitch. After a polite period of time Alex sent the Smitherlys on their way, Mr. Smitherly clutching an envelope containing a lot more than his stated fee.

Shortly after, two neighbour women who did babysitting for Alex and Nancy appeared and divided the herd of kids into two manageable sections, one in the house and one in the smithy.

Alex was resigned to the inevitable, and everybody headed for their cars for a quick trip up the mountain and then along the fire road. They all walked down the path to the campsite, where Alex had erected the tents and readied the fire pit.

Clothing was firing off in all directions while Alex and Nancy headed up to the flat rock from where they traditionally watched the various ceremonies that Saul concocted.

The family came dancing into view, moving to the rhythm of a special chant Saul had put together on the trip up the mountain.

"Different words, Nan, but they still all sound like something from *Jesus Christ Superstar.*"

"That joke is getting a little tired, Alex." A moment later she said, "Doesn't this feel a little strange?"

"What do you mean? It's not much different from all the other ceremonies."

"Well, it seems a little different to me. I have this terrible feeling that by not participating we are slighting our friends—our family. I think we should make the effort."

"You don't mean...tell me you don't mean—"

"I think just this once we should take off our clothes and join them."

"Oh Nancy, I'd like to do this with you. But there's a big problem."

"What are you talking about?"

"I'm talking about something that happens every

time I see you naked. I can't help it and it would be as embarrassing as hell."

"No need to worry about that, boyo. You just stay close to me. I know how to handle the situation. I have fended off hundreds of your early morning unwanted advances, and I can still flick my fingers!"

With that, the newlyweds shed their clothes and walked carefully, hand and hand, down the slope to join their friends.

The rest of the family was overjoyed at their arrival and Alex was made to endure rib cracking sweaty hugs from both Saul and Horst. He managed to maintain his composure when each of the women wrapped their arms around him and squished their breasts into him.

Things were going well and continued after they all paid their respects to the departed and headed back up to the campsite. But then Alex got a glimpse of Nancy, still in the buff, bending over to retrieve a pot from the campfire, and things took a turn for the worse. It was beginning to happen—not yet in a really noticeable fashion, but only seconds away from the Full Monty.

Fortunately Nancy looked up in time. She snapped her fingers and shot a withering glance at the offending appendage, and immediately deflated the crisis. That done, everybody filled their mugs with the camp coffee that they had all come to love and settled in for some more talk about the newlyweds' plans for the future.

Shortly Marina took her leave and headed for her

tent. Then Horst excused himself and followed her. He was only gone for a short time. When he returned, short of breath, he stood beside Dawn. She immediately moved in closer to him, looked up into his eyes, wrapped an arm around him and patted his shoulder with her other hand. It was a 'good boy' sort of pat and it spoke volumes.

In later years, when Alex and Nancy got requests from Horst for slight changes to the dates of the reunion, they didn't have to ask why.

52: Snip, snip

When Nancy gave birth to a healthy, eight-pound baby girl, things had not gone well for her. There were complications and some dangerous moments during the delivery.

Dr. Cruess breathed a sigh of relief when he was able to put things right for her, but he knew he was going to have to advise Nancy that this should be the last pregnancy for her. Another one would be too dangerous, possibly life-threatening.

Alex and Nancy found themselves looking at a future life of careful contraception. "Not my idea of spontaneous fun," he said.

Nancy immediately offered to have her tubes tied, but Alex was not comfortable with that idea. He had been too close to losing her, and wasn't willing to see her under the knife again. It wasn't an easy decision, but he decided that, instead, he would have a vasectomy.

On the morning of the day after he arranged for an appointment with Dr. Cruess, there was a firm knock on the door. Alex opened it to find an irate neighbour. Jack had made another of his moonlight visits to the neighbour's Border Collie bitch. The neighbour said that they had been so securely coupled that the pail of cold water he doused them with had had little effect.

"I'm a reasonable man, Alex, but I've had it. I just got rid of the final mongrel pup from their last encounter and now it looks like I'm in line for another crop. I'm not running a puppy mill! That Jack of yours is a good dog, but you've got to stop him making the rounds and breeding half the females on the mountain."

Alex apologized and felt for his wallet but the man, anticipating what he was about to do, raised his hand to forestall him. "Enough said. I'll be off now. Just see to that dog!"

Alex turned around to see Jack sitting, ears up, with a guilty grin on his face.

"Okay, buddy! You and I are going to have a talk. You have disgraced this family for the last time. You won't put up with being penned in, so there's no other option. I'm going to see Dr. Cruess next week, but you're going to the vet's as soon as I can arrange it."

Dr. Lewis received Jack the same day. He was well aware of the dog's dalliances and had recommended castration last year when he had the dog on his operating table to remove an angry farmer's bird shot pellets from his rump. Like most people who knew Jack, the old vet really liked him. He had managed the whelping of a customer's pure-bred German Shepherd and was so delighted with the quality of the pups that he spoke for one himself.

Alex had to assist the vet with the operation and, knowing what was in store for himself, was extremely empathetic, grimacing at every slice of the knife.

He was having the traditional second thoughts as he said goodbye to Nancy and the kids on his fateful day. He checked Jack closely to assure himself that the dog wasn't suffering any lingering side effects, not as much for the dog's sake as for his own peace of mind. If Jack was showing any adverse symptoms, Alex could still cancel.

He arrived at the outpatients' reception area of the hospital right on time. He didn't want to meet anybody he knew in the waiting room. He hoped the operating room would not be too cold—there would be a female nurse assisting and he wanted to make a good impression.

Alex thought that Dr. Cruess seemed inappropriately jovial as he helped him onto the operating table. "Just lie back and try to relax. I'll give that thing a little freezing, then two quick snips and we'll have you on your way."

They had said that the procedure would be painless, but they were a little optimistic. When the first needle hit a nerve, causing Alex excruciating pain, he unintentionally flung his arm up and backward. It struck a stand holding some medical equipment and sent it flying to the floor.

"C'mon, Alex, watch the equipment! It's expensive," the doctor growled.

"It's not *your* damn equipment I'm concerned

about," was Alex's quick reply.

They both laughed and the rest of the operation went forward without further mishap.

"Oh, c'mon, you two, it's not the end of the world," Nancy chided later in the day. Alex and Jack were sitting side by side on the couch looking injured and forlorn, exchanging sympathetic glances.

53: Fresh footprints

Alex drove the old truck out his driveway and headed up the mountain to his woodlot. It was a practice of his to make sure the 'no hunting' signs were being obeyed. It wasn't that he was against hunting; he was just against hunting without permission.

In particular, he didn't want intruders in the area that was sacred to him. The old family graveyard and the campsite were places he shared with his friends, not with nosy, trespassing hunters.

When he saw the car parked by the path leading from the fire road that marked the northern boundary of his property, he pulled over, got out, and went over for a closer look.

Ontario license plates. The thing is stuffed with junk…looks like somebody has been living in it. I guess I better head over and check. I should have insisted that Jack come with me. The lazy bugger just wanted to keep sleeping beside Nancy. He spends more time with her than me these days.

Alex walked past the inuksuk that marked the entrance to the campsite and headed in.

There were fresh footprints in the path leading

up to the ledge above the graveyard. *Whoever it is must be up there.*

Alex glanced around the campsite. He needed a weapon—something to hold in his hand so whoever was up there would see he meant business. There was a long slender chunk of firewood handy but when he stooped to pick it up, he noticed the six foot length of steel rebar leaning against a tree. It was left over from the cement bake oven he and Saul had constructed.

He picked it up and tested its weight, avoiding its jagged sharp point. Then he moved quietly up the path. *It's probably someone jacking deer. I'll give him a piece of my mind and, if that doesn't work, I'll give him a piece of this.*

Alex gasped with astonishment when he looked down over the ledge. *That's no hunter!*

A man in camouflage fatigues was lying down, adjusting the telescopic sights on a rifle mounted on a tripod.

Jesus, he's pointing that thing at the back of my house!

Alex looked beyond the man, down to where he could just make out the tiny figure of Nancy moving about on their back patio.

54: Slim justice

"It's all about careful planning," Mark Jackson was quietly telling himself. "There's no need for hurry. Everything is in order and ready. I have a good rifle and a magazine full of dumdums that will rip the hell out of them."

He was anticipating a confirming tap on his shoulder and a whispered, 'You're good to go,' from his partner, but when he looked out of the corner of his right eye, no one was there. He wasn't in Afghanistan. He was above the home of a shameless slut, her bastard son and the man who took her from him.

What he was about to do was slim justice, too easy. He would have preferred the kind of punishment prescribed in Afghanistan. Sharia law would have dealt with the slut. She would have been stoned to death and her spawn at the moment of its birth would have been grabbed by the legs and its head bashed against the nearest rock wall.

He would have preferred to have her new man at his disposal for a while so he could use some of the torture techniques he had witnessed before he slowly finished him off with a knife. But this would have to do.

This was the third day he'd lain watching the house. It was always the same. They would always have their breakfast together on the patio. He had the woman clearly in his sights. When the man appeared, he would hit him first, then the woman, then the boy.

A sound of something coming fast up the slope below caught his attention. He looked down to see a snarling German Shepherd running towards him. Without thinking, he lowered the rifle and fired. The animal that was almost through the tombstones below seemed to explode with the impact and flew backwards.

55: On the patio

Nancy, with a cup of coffee in one hand and her laptop in the other, headed for the deck at the rear of the house. She put the coffee down on the patio table, then placed her old MacBook beside it and flipped it open.

Weather permitting, it was a ritual she practised every day. It was her special time to catch up with her friends, and a chance to weigh in on some of the issues that she and other members of the Green Party were attempting to address.

Suddenly the flap of the dog door flew open and a snarling Jack burst out. He ran past her and up the path to the graveyard.

"Oh Jack, you and your bloody squirrels, will you never learn?"

She could hear the dog disappearing in the distance as a tone on the computer signalled it was ready.

"C'mon, baby, show me that the money I spent on the cable was worth it."

Her first message was not what she expected. It was from someone she hadn't heard from in years and she wasn't sure she wanted to read it.

Dearest Nancy

I hope this message finds you well and safe. I think you know by now that your well-being has always been and continues to be a priority with me.

I hope what I'm about to tell you won't trouble you too much and that circumstances will change and make the following information unnecessary, but, as I have done in the past, I choose to err on the side of caution.

As you know I have never really given up on Mark. I prefer to remember him as the young man who I met in your company so long ago.

I have kept track of where he was from his initial incarceration, through the various mental institutions after he was found to be not guilty of his crimes by reason of insanity. He finally landed up at the Oak Ridge branch of the Penetanguishene Mental Health Centre.

He had long since stopped replying to any of my letters or phone calls, but over the years I have been able to talk with the various psychiatrists who were treating him. I was assured that he seemed to be coping with his institutionalization and with treatment and was starting to show improvement.

One thing that they shared with me but kept from you was that under hypnosis Mark revealed that he bore an unreasonable hate for you, Jimmy and me. He considers me a Judas priest and that I and all of my child abusing kind should be put to death. He thinks I betrayed his confession and no amount of telling him that it was several actual witnesses to his heinous crimes that landed him where he now was could change his attitude.

All of this wouldn't matter except that I have just been informed that Mark had shown so much improvement lately that they transferred him to Brockville Psychiatric Hospital, a low security institute.

A week ago, he was granted a day pass. It should have lasted only three hours, but he never returned; instead a local Catholic priest was found near the altar of his church, badly beaten and left for dead.

The RCMP has issued an all-points—

The crack of a rifle shot echoed down the mountain.

56: No time for words

Alex, startled by the shot, hesitated for a moment. He saw the man quickly adjusting the range on his rifle, then realized what was happening.

He took three strides forward and hurled the rebar like a javelin. It hit the man in the soft flesh below his right shoulder and embedded itself.

The man screamed and leapt to his feet, sending his rifle and tripod sailing over the edge of the outcrop. He circled twice, trying to reach back and dislodge the rebar, but the movement only served to embed it deeper.

Pushing Alex aside, the man ran down the path to the camp, with the free end of the iron rod scoring the dirt in his wake. Alex didn't follow him. He had to get to Jack.

He found the dog lying lifeless beside Ben Johnson's grave. There was a small entrance wound where the bullet had entered his chest, but the bullet had torn through his lower body.

"Oh, Jack, I'm so sorry, boy, but I've got to leave you here. I've got to get down to Nancy and Jimmy." He looked at his great-grandfather's tombstone. "You're in good hands, old guy, don't worry."

Alex set off running full tilt down the slope toward his house, tumbling, falling, and recovering over and over. In minutes that seemed like hours he finally made it to where an astonished Nancy was standing with their breakfast tray.

There was no time for words. He grabbed her in his arms, sending the tray flying, and steered her in the back door.

"Where's Jimmy?

"What? He just went into the bathroom."

"I'll explain later. Call 911. Say, 'Man with a gun'."

Alex ran back up the path to where he had left Jack. The granite surface of his great-grandfather's tombstone was smeared with blood.

Jack seemed unconscious, but his legs were flailing in an involuntary fashion and he was breathing. Alex rolled him over, revealing again the long slash along his back from shoulder to rump. The wound seemed deeper in places and blood was flowing quickly from those areas.

"Oh, Jesus, Jack, hang on!"

Alex scooped the heavy dog up in his arms. He folded the proud flesh of the sides of the wound together, placing his hands directly on top of the deeper spots in an effort to stem the flow of blood, and set off at a staggering run down the slope toward the house.

The front of his shirt was turning red but there was less bleeding than he expected. Not wanting to fall and cause his dog further injury he slowed his pace until he reached the back of his house.

Nancy, looking frantic, was standing with Jimmy in hand and Lucie on her hip when he finally staggered onto the rear deck. "You and the kids get into the car. You drive. We've got to get over to Doctor Lewis. I'll explain later. Call 911 again and tell them what we're doing."

It was lucky that the doctor was in his surgery. As soon as he saw Alex with Jack in his arms, he ushered him directly into his operating room.

"I'm on my own today. I'm afraid you're going to have to help me. I hope you're not going to be squeamish like the last time."

Jack was quietly whining now. Alex gently put the dog on the table and unwrapped his arms, displaying the extent of the injury.

"Jesus, what a mess. What the hell happened? Never mind, tell me later, I've got to get on with this."

The doctor rushed to his medicine cabinet and grabbed a syringe and a vial of barbiturate. The effect of the injection was immediate and Jack fell instantly limp.

While Alex steadied the dog, the vet intubated him. "I'll use this to deliver some further anaesthetic."

He clipped a pulse-oximeter sensor to the dog's tongue. "This rig measures oxygen saturation in the hemoglobin, and the pulse. Watch those numbers on that monitor. If the oxygen falls below this mark, turn that oxygen knob to the right for more. You're on your own now; I've got to get on with this."

It was an endless time of trying to be helpful

without really knowing what he could do. Alex kept staring at the monitor, willing the numbers to stay good. He barely noticed when paramedics, and then RCMP officers, appeared; his focus was all on Jack. He had no idea if his answers to their questions made any sense at all.

It took the better part of two hours for Doc Lewis to painstakingly clean, cauterize and stitch up the gruesome wound. Alex had not allowed himself to believe that it would really be possible for such extensive damage to be repaired; but as the operation progressed, he began to hope.

Then, in a flash, that hope disintegrated when the lines on the monitor dropped and the alarm began beeping, showing no pulse and zero oxygen.

It was the same sound that the monitors made when his grandfather died back in that hospital in Toronto.

His dog was dead, and he was instantly overcome with grief.

Doc Lewis had finished inserting a temporary drain tube to the lower end of the wound and was feeling pretty proud of himself.

When he saw how Alex was reacting to the sounds coming from the monitor, he pushed him aside and reattached the clip to Jack's tongue. The monitor instantly reverted to its normal status.

"I thought I told you to watch that thing, Alex. I think everything is going to be all right, but I'll have to keep him here for a couple of days to be sure. You get out to Nancy and the kids now. They need you."

57: Prize student

Alex was sitting alone at the breakfast table, nursing his coffee, as he finally dared to read the four-day-old newspaper that he had been avoiding. He had gone to the veterinary clinic first thing in the morning to pick up a groggy but apparently recovering Jack. There would be a few days before the stitches could be removed, but Dr. Lewis felt that the dog would be happier at home.

Jimmy was sitting by the dog bed with Jack's head on his lap and Lucie had dragged out her toy stethoscope and was playing nurse, giving Jack a thorough examination.

Alex had just unfolded the paper to the second page and was beginning to read when he heard Nancy coming down the stairs. He quickly closed the paper up, but not quickly enough.

"What are you reading?" she mumbled. She was still experiencing the drowsy effects of the tranquilizers Dr. Cruess had recommended she take for a few days.

"You don't need to know. You've been through enough. I'll throw this thing in the trash."

"You'll do no such thing. Let's get this madness

over with. Read it to me or I'll read it myself."

Alex got Nancy a cup of coffee, sat her down where they would be out of earshot of the children, and reopened the paper. "It looks like they pretty much reprinted the media release the Mounties sent out, plus some witness quotes."

> On July 27, 2008 units of the Kingston Detachment of the RCMP responded to a 911 emergency call from a woman who said that there had been an attempt on her life. She said that the assailant was last seen on a fire road on the North Mountain near Middleton. Her current husband provided a description of the suspect's car.
>
> An Amber Alert was immediately issued, saying shots were fired, describing the suspect, and cautioning everyone that he was armed and dangerous and should not be approached.
>
> Officers found a high-powered telescopic rifle and a spent shell casing below a rock ledge overlooking the rear of the home of the couple who phoned 911.
>
> A vehicle fitting the description of the suspect's car was found abandoned in front of the Catholic Church on the CFB Greenwood Base. The driver's seat was soaked in blood.
>
> Military Police personnel immediately established a cordon around the church and awaited further reinforcements from RCMP.

Two parishioners who had been meeting with Father Patrick Crosby at the chapel confirmed that the priest was still in the church.

Sergeant Crawford of the RCMP assumed command of what now appeared to be a hostage taking.

Alex looked up. "How can an RCMP officer take precedence over the MPs on a military base?"

"Just read the story," Nancy said. She was sitting very still, hands clasped.

The sergeant attempted to make contact with Jackson or Crosby, but there was no response.

When sounds of a struggle were heard, the sergeant sent two of his men, who were qualified as sharpshooters, to suitable vantage points to cover the two doors to the church.

At the suggestion of Lieutenant Colonel Anderson, Base Commander of 14 Wing Greenwood, he detailed a qualified member of the Military Police to take a third position at a distance.

When the sergeant made another attempt to speak with Jackson or the priest, a shot was fired from the interior of the church, exiting through the glass across the top of the front door.

A few moments later the front doors opened and Father Crosby appeared with the assailant behind him. The assailant appeared to be holding a pistol and was heard to say, 'Now you're all going to see what happens to a Judas priest who betrays his vows.'

A witness at the scene later stated, "Before the man could pull the trigger, he was suddenly flung backwards. The priest was not injured, but the assailant was declared dead at the scene.

Chief Warrant Officer Don Leblanc, the third man positioned to cover the doors, fired the shot that saved the priest's life—"

Nancy broke out in tears. "Oh my God, oh my God. Can this get any worse?"

Alex slipped around the table and leaned over Nancy's chair, embracing her. "What is it, Nan, what is it, what is it?"

After gulping several deep breathes she was finally able to speak. "Don...Don Leblanc. Don was Mark's prize student. He ate countless dinners with us. Mark always referred to him as the kid with a keen eye and nerves of steel who would someday make his country proud."

58: I won't pull any punches

Doctor Cruess had prescribed a mild tranquilizer to settle Nancy's fractured nerves and help her sleep, but he decided, considering the complexity of her problem, to refer her to Dr. Gower, a psychiatrist friend of his who was particularly good at grief counselling. The aging doctor had performed countless sympathetic supportive sessions with military widows.

Nancy was adamant that Alex should be present at her appointments and Dr. Gower agreed. "The more support, the better."

The first sessions, for some of which she agreed to be hypnotized, dealt with her deeply-ingrained sense of guilt that she had at being somehow responsible for what Mark had become and what he had done; but shortly they morphed into something immediate and of more concern.

"There is nothing anyone can do to help Mark now, Doctor, but what about Jimmy? How do I ever tell him about his father and how he died, and how will all this affect him? I've read that what you refer to as Mark's psychopathy can be inherited. Is that true? Tell me that that isn't true!"

"Let's not get ahead of ourselves here, my dear. It's not that simple. Let me explain and I won't pull any punches."

Nancy and Alex pushed back into their green leather chairs and listened anxiously.

"Psychopathy is characterized by diagnostic features such as superficial charm, high intelligence, poor judgment, a failure to learn from experience—"

"But that's not Mark," Nancy interrupted. "That's not the way he was."

"Not the way he was, but that was what he became. Let me continue to see if we can shed some light on the situation. There is no 'psychopathic gene', but research tells us that psychopathy tends to run in families. Even if a parent does not have psychopathy, they may carry one or more genetic variants that increase their child's chance of developing psychopathy.

"Oh my God, so you're saying Jimmy could—"

"No, no, no! It's more complicated than that. No one is born with psychopathy, or any other psychological disorder. However, some children are born at high risk for developing psychopathy due to inherited factors."

"And that's my Jimmy you're talking about?"

"Not at all. I told you I wouldn't pull any punches and I'm not, but all I've given you so far is the bad news. It's not all bad news. Environmental influences can change the odds of developing psychopathy in people who are at risk due to inherited factors. Some children are born at higher risk for psychopathy due to genetic variables that affect brain development. But parents still play an important role. Learning to use specific therapeutic techniques with high-risk children can reduce their chances of developing psychopathy."

The doctor looked from Nancy to Alex and back, to make sure they were following him. "Remember that a risk factor is not the same as a cause. In a situation like Jimmy's, even if he could inherit a genetic trait, and we don't know that, nurture more than compensates for the dangers of nature. Warm and responsive parenting is what he needs, and I know you two are up to the task."

Alex said, "When and how do you suggest we tell Jimmy about his father and how he died?"

"When he asks, and do it truthfully. And only answer the question he asks. In time, as he gets older, he will ask for more details."

59: What book is that?

"Good morning, Mr. Johnson, my name is Danny Arseneau. I guess I should have called ahead."

Oh crap, another Jehovah's Witness, and a British one at that. When are they going to give up on me?

Aloud, Alex said, "Well, Mr. Arseneau, you're wasting your time. But the coffee is on, so you better come in and give it your best shot."

Danny, a little confused by his reception, followed Alex into the kitchen, took a chair at the table and accepted a cup of coffee.

"So what's on your mind this morning, Danny? Is it all right if I call you Danny? You must be new to the area."

"It's about a book, Mr. Johnson," Danny offered tentatively.

"Oh, the Book! Yup, got it: the Holy Scriptures right up there on that bookshelf and I keep getting copies of *The Watchtower* and *Awake* in the mail. I think I have all the books I need."

Danny began to chuckle and almost spilled his coffee. "I *really* should have called ahead. I'm not a— you know, whatever you think I am. I wanted to talk to you about *my* book."

Now Alex was confused. "Your book. What book is that?"

"Well, it's not a book yet. But maybe, with your help, it will be one day. I'm calling it 'Royal Wild Oats'."

"I think you have come to the wrong door, Danny, agronomy is not on my list of talents."

The two men looked up as the kitchen door swung open and Nancy entered the room. "Any of that coffee left?" she asked while giving their visitor the quick once-over.

"Help yourself. This is Danny and he is not a missionary. It seems he got some wrong directions and I was about to refer him to the Department of Agriculture in Kentville."

"Good to meet you, Danny. I'm about to make some breakfast. Could I interest you in some scrambled eggs, fresh from the coop this morning?"

"That sounds great, Mrs. Johnson, but first I think I better explain something. I didn't come to the wrong door."

Alex wasn't pleased that Nancy had extended the invitation to breakfast, particularly since he didn't like the ominous tone of Danny's last sentence.

Danny continued, "I'm a journalist, and before I began this project, I worked for several years for the *Yorkshire Tribune*."

"Project! What project?" Alex exclaimed. "What on earth has this got to do with us?"

"If you let me explain, Alex, ah, Mr. Johnson, I think that you will find that my project has a great deal to do with you in particular."

Nancy busied herself with breakfast preparations, keeping one ear on the conversation.

Danny said, "Let me start by saying that Alex and I have some shared family history that Alex doesn't know about, and that I only recently discovered myself. Several years ago I discovered four old letters that my father had saved from my grandfather's belongings. He didn't leave much else, because he never had a permanent home. He was always on the move. He was a gypsy or, as we call them, a traveller. What I read in one of those letters was the beginning of my book project and what has led me to your door."

Nancy said, "I think I'm going to cook this after you are finished your story. I wouldn't want breakfast to get cold."

Danny threw her a quick smile. "Three of the four letters came from here, from this house where we now sit. They are filled with lots of interesting gossip and news from around this area. I believe your great-grandmother, Lilly Johnson, wrote them on behalf of *my* great-grandmother, Angeline Arseneau."

Alex said, "I know of your Angeline. Those two were close."

"The three letters were fascinating and I treasure them, but the letter that got my full attention was the one that my great-grandmother wrote herself. The script is crude and there are frequent spelling errors, but it made its point. The contents shocked me. I had to know more."

"Know more about what?"

Danny seemed a little embarrassed. "I should explain that the book I am working on exposes centuries of misconduct on the part of the British royal family. There are hundreds of examples of the dalliances of kings, princes and other male members of the nobility, but almost all of the known instances involve influential families that benefited from the relationships. For instance, did you know that Edward VII, while still the Prince of Wales, initiated an affair with Alice Keppel that continued during his marriage to Queen Alexandra, and that Alice Keppel is the great-grandmother of Camilla Parker Bowles? Camilla is now the Duchess of Cornwall, the wife of the Prince of Wales. Only a DNA test could determine how close their relationship is."

"They won't let that happen," Alex said.

"No. But isn't it nice how these things work out for certain people? My book is more about the multitude of women, mostly lower class, whom the royals have victimized and then tossed aside. I mention Edward VII because he played a major role in the story I need to share with you."

Danny drained his coffee cup, which Nancy swiftly refilled.

"I consulted the military records of my grandfather, Tommy Arseneau. I found out that he served with the West Nova Regiment during WWI, and that his friend, Danny Johnson, served alongside him. They both gave their home address as being this house, which confirmed the close relationship suggested in Lilly Johnson's letters."

Alex felt prickles down his spine. This fairy-tale story about princes and gypsies suddenly had his grandfather in it!

"You said the letter your great-grandmother wrote shocked you," Nancy said. "What was in it?"

Danny looked around the room. "Is this indeed the house where our grandfathers were boyhood friends and lived together?"

"Close," Alex said. "The foundation is the same, but I had to build new. It looks pretty much the same on the outside."

He pointed to the framed photo on the wall "That's the original house in the background. I think Nancy and I did a pretty good job of replicating it. If what you say is true, the boy on the left in that picture is my grandfather and the one on the right is yours."

Danny Arseneau pushed out his chair, got to his feet slowly, and moved in for a closer look. He stood transfixed for a long time. This was more than he could have ever hoped for.

Nancy waited a while and then interrupted his reverie. "Are you all right? Maybe you should sit down again."

Danny complied, fidgeting with his glasses. "It's odd, but I feel sort of at home here. I thought it was going to be uncomfortable to share what I found out in that letter, but now it seems like it was something that I was meant to do. So I'll get on with it. Our great-grandmothers were best friends. They met while they were both maids at, um, the Spa Springs Hotel before it burned. Is that your understanding, Alex?"

"That's what my grandfather told me."

"Well, since everything you have said and shown me confirms what I believed and hoped, I had better get down to it. I mentioned Edward VII. He, more than any other person, is responsible for my visit. I learned from the letter that in 1890, just before the Spa Springs Hotel burned down, the then Prince of Wales was in residence. Something that I find hard to talk about occurred that upset my great-grandmother immensely."

"Whoa!" Alex said. "No wonder you're upset and on a crusade. You're suggesting that the Prince, true to form, wandered below stairs and took advantage of your great gram?"

"I'm afraid you misunderstand me, Alex. My great-grandmother wrote that the Prince of Wales raped Lilly Johnson, who would have been fifteen years old, in his room at the hotel. The result was the child later known as Danny Johnson."

Garry Leeson

60: The strange case of Daniel Johnson

Berlin 2005

The Canadian government acknowledged the contributions Pieter Martin had made entitled him to a substantial severance package, and told the press that he was now officially retired to Germany. But how do you simply retire an inquiring mind?

Pieter was ninety years old, a ground-breaking geneticist who had devoted his whole life to the practical application of the new scientific discipline he had encountered when he was a student at the university in Munich in 1968. By then Philip Leder's discovery of a way to decipher the 64 RNA three-letter code of amino acids was old news, but for Pieter it was just the beginning of a lifelong quest.

Over his years in Canada, he had provided forensic evidence to solve crimes, testified at paternity trials and aided in many other DNA dependent inquiries. The scientific detective work suited him and the type of curiosity it required was not something that he could simply turn off.

He was going over some of his old files, and found

one of the more unusual things that had come to light in Nova Scotia. A friend of his assistant, Horst Anderson, had given him a sample, the results of which did not match up with what Pieter knew of the donor's circumstances and probable heredity. He recalled how unusual it had been. But at the time Pieter's workload was so heavy, that he had had to set the file aside for later.

And now it was 'later'. He now had all the time in the world to play with the puzzle.

Pieter reviewed the suspicious results of the test of Alex Johnson and decided that a reliable confirmation of what was going on sat waiting in the unopened envelope from the Valour Project he had brought with him from Canada. He had asked for assistance from the institute, but had not had the time to investigate the results before returning to Germany. A great deal of time had elapsed since then.

The large German portion of Alex Johnson's DNA, that had surprised him when he first discovered it, was many times stronger in the results submitted by the Valour Project for Alex's grandfather. This was unusual for a person of Maritime Canadian heritage, and the very typical blueprint for someone from continental Great Britain.

Pieter compared the two results further. An idea was beginning to take shape. He was recalling another DNA chart he had once seen. It didn't make sense, but these two sets of results had the same components as the results for Queen Elizabeth II.

A crazy notion took hold of Pieter. *There could be*

a real relationship. If I can somehow prove it, it would mark a fitting end to my career.

The proof of the pudding would come from the type of research a team of scientists had used in identifying remains as those of the last Czar of Russia and his immediate family. Most of the exhumed bones had carried the infamous Hemophilia B gene on their X chromosomes that could be traced back to Queen Victoria.

Pieter could have applauded himself for his cleverness when, after discretely obtaining a more detailed examination of Daniel Johnson's DNA, he found the same mutation, but he chose not to celebrate. What good would it do? Who would the information help? Who would it hinder? He chose rather to sit on the information. Why risk sullying his legacy with something like the farcical episode involving Anastasia?

He was often asked to dinner at the family home of the Andersons and couldn't restrain himself from plying his former assistant, Horst, with subtle questions about Alex. He would say inane, out-of-the-blue things like, 'So, Horst, did your friend Alex ever mention that there was hemophilia in his family?" Horst and Dawn would stare at each other incredulously and dismiss the question as just evidence of their old friend's worsening dementia. while trying to find an appropriate response.

So Pieter Martin had all but decided to keep his discovery to himself. *At my age, that shouldn't be too long.*

But fate had something else in store for him. The next time he was invited to the Andersons for dinner, amid the pleasant conversation there was a most unusual disclosure.

"I have a story to tell you, Dr. Martin," Horst said, "and a copy of a most unusual letter that has been shared with me. Maybe you should read the letter first."

The old man dug out his reading glasses and began to read. When he finished he looked up with a satisfied smile on his face.

"This information is shocking," Horst said. "Why do you seem so pleased?"

"Sit back, children. I have a tale to tell."

61: Find the right words

June 6, 2022

It was Alex's birthday, and he was looking into his bathroom mirror to assess the damage the decades had inflicted.

Fifty years! Jesus, where has the time gone? Nancy is only two years younger than me, but she sure looks a lot better than me. She's still got her figure and those awesome legs. Her birthday treat in bed last night was wonderful, just like the good old days, but I'm not the man I used to be, that's for sure.

His email inbox was filled with birthday wishes from family members who had spread out all over the globe: Australia, British Columbia, Germany, New York, and, of course, Ontario.

What a difference the past thirty years have made, and how different they would have been if I had simply spread my grandfather's ashes and immediately headed back to Toronto.

There was a lot of water under the bridge since those days. Who would have thought that Marina and Horst would fall in love, get married and move to Germany, or that Heather would come to terms with being gay and end up having one of the first same-sex weddings in North America? But most surprising was that Saul had completely reverted to the lifestyle he had abandoned, and was at the reins of his family business. He and Marina were living happy and contented in the Big Apple.

Despite the radical changes, everybody had remained fast friends and looked forward to their annual reunions.

Alex could hear Nancy moving around down in the kitchen, so he flipped open his daily pill planner and gulped down his meds. He descended the stairs slowly, conscious of his new knee replacement, then paused at the kitchen door and gazed at Nancy.

She had left the lights off and she was standing by the window, holding a basket of eggs and talking quietly through the window to her favourite hen, who was perched on the outside sill. The morning sun highlighted her features and made the eggs glow through the lattice of the basket. The scene was surreal. He wished he had his camera with him.

Alex and Nancy would not be hosting the family's annual summer reunion in person this year. It would be too dangerous with the COVID pandemic wreaking havoc among even the conscientious, three-time vaxxers that he knew his friends were. They had had to cancel it the previous year as well after not missing the annual event once since 1990.

Yesterday, they had strolled through the old campsite on the mountain, remembering all the warm, crazy things that had occurred there over the years and missing their old friends terribly.

Horst had arranged for everybody to meet remotely on Zoom today. It would be better than nothing and, since their internet connection had been recently upgraded, they hoped that they wouldn't have to suffer the anguish of seeing their friends frequently pixilate, freeze, and temporarily disappear this time.

Horst was managing the whole thing from his and Dawn's home in Germany, Saul and Marina would participate from New York City and Heather and her partner, Lisa, from their apartment in Toronto.

Back in 1990 none of them could have imagined the sorry state they now found the world in. They had bought into the notion that they were witnessing the dawn of the age of Aquarius, and had been full of hope. But the ideal world they thought they had created only bloomed for a very short time before reality kicked in and all of them, each in their own fashion, had to revert to some version of the lifestyles they had rejected. Once a year, for a few precious days, everybody would come with their offspring in tow and try to recapture at least a fragment of the feeling of freedom they had once possessed.

Alex moved the couch and positioned the computer so that, when they were seated, they would be centred in the square that would soon pop up on the screen.

A last minute readjustment had become necessary when Tilly, their Border Collie/Sheltie cross pup, decided that she wanted to be part of the family portrait. She was the third successive addition to their kennel since faithful old Jack had passed away.

Nancy slipped off the couch, went to the computer, and signed in. They were the first, but Alex had indicated that he wanted to use all the time available because, after they dispensed with all the news about what was happening in their lives and what their children were up to, he had something very important to share with them. All the children, except his and Nancy's offspring, shared Horst as their biological father, a situation that everybody involved was comfortable with. They were always anxious for each other's company, but today their participation would clutter up the screen with too many squares and too much chatter.

One by one the boxes on the screen opened to reveal their friends peering into their cameras and making adjustments.

Horst opened the proceedings by rendering the German version of Happy Birthday in his deep baritone voice. The squares that were unmuted broke out in laughter while the others pantomimed their approval.

Alex enjoyed the first half hour of back and forth with his friends, but was anxious to bring up something he felt was more important and that they all would want to weigh in on. He raised his hand and waved to get everybody's attention.

Then he hit unmute and picked up a sheet of paper that had been resting on his lap. "I got this email from Dan Arseneau yesterday and I'd like to read it to you and get your opinions."

I hope the letter finds you and yours well. Things are shitty over here and I understand that they are not much better where you are. However, given the choice, I think I might opt for Spa Springs over London.

I have some good news as well as some bad news. I'll commence with the good news. After an eternity of editing and rewriting, "Royal Wild Oats" went to the printer, and the publisher received the first four copies for final approval. I'll receive one copy, a second is in the mail for you, the publisher keeps one copy and—now for the bad news—the fourth has long since been in the hands of the Royal Communications Office. They have been unusually prompt in their response.

The letter the publisher received, with the Palace letterhead, began with the dreaded "Without Prejudice".

Apparently, the Queen was not amused and her reply concerning the chapters involving your great grandfather, Danny Johnson, was unequivocal: 'I do feel most definitely that those chapters should not be included.'

The Palace lawyers suggest that the information regarding the Prince of Wales' activities in the 1890s is scurrilous and unfounded, and that we should not release the book.

You may already know this, but it is unlawful to use the word 'Royal' anywhere in the Commonwealth without the Queen's permission. Strangely there was no objection to the title of the book, only the portion concerning your grandfather.

To be fair, our beloved old Queen has had a rough go of it lately. It seemed like everybody and their uncle was making a less than complimentary movie or TV show about her, Prince Harry and his wife abandoned their post, and then she lost Prince Philip. But why, assuming that she was personally aware of the chapters concerning the misbehaviour of her grandfather, would she object? The objection sounds like the work of an overzealous junior assistant at the Cabinet Office.

More probably the striking similarity of something that happened with The Prince of Wales in 1890 to a situation with one of the current royals is what has caught their attention.

My publisher is content to leave the book as is and his legal team is preparing a rebuttal for the Cabinet Office. They are confident in their position, but have asked me to ask you, a person centrally concerned, to respond to their request to expunge the chapters personally and deny any provable connection with the Royal Family.

I'm sure that you will find the right words. Send them to me and I'll pass them along."

Looking directly at the screen, Alex said, "And so I did."

At that, the square framing Horst lit up and he burst out, "We have all the proof. Tell me you're not going to let them bully you. What did you reply?"

Alex paused, restraining himself momentarily, before answering, letting his great-grandmother's words play over and over in his head. "Royal bastards are ghosts best forgotten, royal bastards are ghosts best forgotten."

When he couldn't contain himself further, he blurted out gleefully, "I said to tell those pompous, interfering pricks at the Palace that the story stays, and that, if they didn't like it, they could kiss my Royal ass!"

At that the whole family broke into uncontrollable laughter that lasted as, one by one, the squares disappeared.

Dan Johnson's Ashes

Garry Leeson

Acknowledgements

Without the amazing assistance of my editor, Andrew Wetmore, the encouragement of Moose House Publication's founder Brenda Thompson, and the artistic talent of Rebekah Wetmore, this book would not exist.

About the author

Garry Leeson is an award-winning author, playwright, auctioneer, and by times, logger and farmer, from the Annapolis Valley in Nova Scotia. His works have appeared in periodicals in Canada and USA; his plays have had productions in Kentville and Lunenburg, and CBC Radio has showcased his short stories.

He was long-listed for CBC Writes in the Creative Nonfiction category in 2012. He was a recipient of an Arts Nova Scotia grant and in 2020 received the Margaret and John Savage First Book Award for Non-Fiction for his book, *The Dome Chronicles*.

Garry lives with his wife, Andrea, and a menagerie of animals, in the community of Harmony.

For the curious of mind, visit garryleeson.com

Garry Leeson

Book club discussion guide

Here are some questions you can use for jumping-off points as you discuss *Dan Johnson's Ashes.*

1. **Literary Minimalism** refers to writing with a small, specific focus, usually without flowery, excessively descriptive language and backstory, prioritizing brevity and allowing the reader to make up for a lack of details with their imagination. Were you able to fill in the story's details of setting, sounds, and how the characters look? Would you have preferred more descriptions of where things happened and what people looked like?

2. What was your impression of Dan Johnson when we meet him in his hospital room on his 100th birthday?

3. Did his conversations with his grandson Alex and what the hospital staff said about him change your opinion?

4. Some Canadian WWI veterans, like John Henry Foster and Harry Patch, lived to 109. Was it realistic to make the fictional Dan Johnson 100?

5. The Valour Project's collection of DNA from war heroes is a figment of the author's imagination. If it was really happening, why would it be a good or a bad project?

6. Dan and his grandson Alex have a lot of fiery conversations. What do they really feel about each other?

7. Was it useful to have Jack the dog as an important character? What does Alex's relationship with Jack reveal about his character? Are Jack's actions at key points in the story realistic?

8. Do the characters connected to the old blacksmith shop and the town of Middleton remind you of anyone?

9. Are Saul and his family of sister-wives in a believable relationship typical of the flower power movement of the hippie era?

10. Is it better to read *The Secret of the Spring* first to fully appreciate *Dan Johnson's Ashes*, or can you read this book without the other one?

11. Do you think this book makes an unfair attack on the Royal Family, or does what we know of the way past Royal Family members have acted make the author's speculation reasonable?

12. How would the family tree of the kings and
    queens of England look if it included all their
    illegitimate children?
    You can search online for charts of the official
    family tree of the House of Windsor, such as
    the extensive one at wikipedia.org (search on
    "British royal family tree").